X in Paris

X in Paris

by Michael Brodsky

Four Walls Eight Windows, New York

Copyright© 1988 Michael Brodsky

First paperback edition published by:
  Four Walls Eight Windows
  Post Office Box 548
  Village Station
  New York, New York 10014

"The Tenement" first appeared in *Dyslexia;* "A Day
in the Life of an Uninvited Guest" first appeared in
Sun; "Origin" first appeared in *The Portable Lower
East Side.* Grateful acknowledgement is made for
permission to reprint these.

Library of Congress Cataloging-in-Publication Data

Brodsky, Michael, 1948-
  X in Paris/by Michael Brodsky.
    p.   cm.
  ISBN 0-941423-13-1 (pbk.): $9.95
  I. Title.
PS3552.R6233X15 1988   88-16034
813'.54—dc19   CIP

Manufactured in the U.S.A.

Table of Contents

X in Paris

I arrive in Paris late one night and go to a hotel not far from the one I stayed at two years before. Why Paris. Paris is an exercise in despair, Paris is the workshop or rather the quarry whence I extract raw materials to be worked, later, into a coherence acceptable to what I perceive as the laws of my vocation. I note a few American girls being talked to by a young man who does not move his arms like an American. The American girl is unmistakable. She listens smugly skeptical, half or three quarters of her attention already clawing toward an elsewhere, the something better just around the corner. The hotel clerk looks at me with a calm that contrasts starkly with the anguish I begin to unload. Before I turn on the light I am already resisting what I perceive of the room's contour. The next day I begin what I have, in part, come to Paris for. I have come to Paris to pursue what bears the configuration of a shameless activity. We will call it X. I need not specify, specification will only obstruct the elaboration of a network of relations, connections, to which X lends itself easily enough when unencumbered by, depopulated of, specific features, ubiquitous nuances. So unencumbered X becomes my foothold in, pretext for, thought, or rather thoughts, since my capacity to survive is dependent on their increase. X is the theater of my anguish. This means that this anguish is estranged in, displaced to, X. This means that once submitted to X, to the protocol of X, I undergo my anguish, my despair, only in the form of a perpetual conflict between resistance and surrender to X. The conflict breeds thoughts. In return for undergoing the full weight of my despair as a human animal in X—for railroading my despair to the domain of X—I acquire thoughts, thoughts about being. But thoughts about being come to me—indemnification is allowed me—only after I have shown myself willing to submit to collision after collision with the tenuous protocol of X. So indemnified, with thoughts, I can go on. I acquire thoughts, therefore I am. *Acquire* is the key here. Very early the next morning I buy the weekly listing the significant events of the week. I feel I should visit the museums, attend the respectably important film and theater events. For whatever enrichment comes from X—of course I anticipate a future, retrospective enrichment but deep in the domain of X or even on the margin of that domain enrichment is inconceivable—is axiomatically illegitimate, frenetically disordered, far outside computability. I sit on a bench. For summer it is cold and drizzly. Parisians are on their way to work. I debate whether to have breakfast in a cafe or spend fourteen francs on breakfast in the hotel. It could very well turn out copious enough to permit my going without food well on into the late afternoon.

I am here, in Paris. For so long I have been anticipating this visit. But, a ravenous anticipation never took into account my own participation, inevitably, in the spectacle anticipated. I never considered what the reality would be once infiltrated with my concreteness, the concreteness of my warring needs and primordial sorrows, my waking odors and secretions. Anticipation of participation is always delicious because it is always spared a preview of the participant's symptoms. I rise from the bench. These benches at the edge of the wide pavement fill me with delight. Two wings separated by a partition. And there is always a handsome plane tree nearby, its roots put to rest beneath a perfectly circular grate.

Having left wife and son on the small island where her family continues to spend its summer vacation I am on the verge of being overwhelmed by despair. Is this despair at, in, separation

2

the cause of or the pretext for re-immersion in X. "Is this despair at, in . . . ," this is a sample of the kind of indemnifying thought I await.

My son stood on shore with his mother and waved and waved and waved at the retreating prow. On the train from Nantes to Paris I found myself sitting across from a thin, middle-aged woman with a worried shrivelled face, smoking. She was not, contrary to my fears, in the least revolted by my nibbling surreptitiously and absolutely without appetite at the cheese sandwiches, grapefruit and *pain au chocolat* solicitously packed just before departure. As long as I could reassure myself about the accumulated tortures awaiting me upon return to New York—from job, coworkers, bosses, burglars, and from the stalemate which had long before joined forces with my vocation—I felt comfortable on ferry, bus and train. The inevitability of future pain was something solid to oppose to the partial obliterations inevitable once I placed myself in the hands of the city of light. On the bus to Nantes from Fromentine I found myself hungering after the anguish undergone two years previous, when I had left wife and son in Brive for the same destination in order to get a few days' headstart on our projected brief sojourn together before the tumult of Roissy. I found myself hungering for a recrudescence of that anguish because now, at a distance, it seemed airtight, secure, eminently enviable. Then it had been, doubtless, as massive and as clandestine as the version just about to spring but now there was no intrusion of a writhing physiognomy—no intrusion of a symptom-laden concreteness—to mar the contemplation of what, serene and devoutly to be wished, flashed forth the surety of its own concludedness replete. with beginning and middle in addition to end. This remembered anguish was nothing less than the only legitimate—the only conceivable—anguish. But I was incapable of clothing myself in such borrowed finery since I was clearly not the being of two years before. Somewhere in the space between the first paroxysm

3

and this second taking its time about unfolding I had altered. Hearing a cat mewling in the back of the bus I felt myself on the verge of a thought. The thought told me it was not so much separation and departure and its aftermath that was about to torture me as the freshly intuited tension between the hunger to undergo present anguish as the exact facsimile of retroactively paradigmatic anguish past—or rather the hunger to undergo present being as anguish in some form, in other words in its only conceivable legitimate form, that of anguish already over and done with—AND the impossibility of thrashing past the barrier of an inurement, an evolution in the interval between present, past. The thought did not give up: It was not so much despair at separation that was about to be undergone as an agonizing confusion over the nature—name, rank and serial number—of what was at present unfolding or about to unfold. What was it. It certainly did not resemble, from where I sat, despair in its paradigmatic form. I played back the thought. The thought stated that it was not so much despair at separation that was being undergone . . . not so much despair at separation that was being undergone . . . not so much . . . but this was absurd. But I was too happy with my acquisition to take issue with its content. The thought had spoken with authority. I knew without articulating that if the thought was to qualify as a precious acquisition, an affirmation of persistence in my own being, an encapsulated dramatic event, an undergoable convulsion, then it must embody the supersession of one state of affairs—the obvious, the incontrovertible—by another. The obvious state of affairs was simple anguish at being separated from those I loved. But what could that state of affairs yield me but anguish. Could submission to that state of affairs indemnify me in some way. In the plane of thought it was possible to avenge myself on the state of affairs for the state of affairs. Only in the plane of thought. In the plane of thought the one, the only, state of affairs, in submitting to certain tricks of syntax, relinquished its preeminence. its incontrovertibility.

The thought told me it was not anguish at separation that I was enduring but . . . Not A but B. In the plane of thought my indemnification for undergoing A was a thought—was the acquisition of a thought—in which the shelving, the denigration, the supersession of A was secured for all eternity. But only in the plane of thought for as I descended from the bus and struggled to remove my duffel bag, brown and green, stashed in the hold I felt myself being felled into permanent inconsolability by a particular slant of sun on the white wall of the *gare*.

The next day, after the copious fourteen franc hotel breakfast, I take the métro. Having bought a *carnet* the night before I am sure to save a considerable amount of money. Two years before tickets were purchased only one by one. This tactic had denied any fixed duration to a sojourn scheduled to last the several days until my wife's arrival. This time I am accepting the fact of a fixed duration by adopting the rational maneuvers appropriate for making it most agreeable even though at every moment, or at every other moment, my state of mind implies immediate departure. By buying a *carnet* I eliminate the need for frequent transactions with ticketsellers under glass, I no longer count on those spasms of connectedness to postpone by obliteration. In spite of my grief I have succeeded in resolving the problem of whether I ought to make myself responsible for my own being, my own foul-smelling parcel of reality, or disseminate it among a host of curtly efficient functionaries. Yet at the same time I loathe this proof of a progress, an evolution, a . . . rehabilitation. Surrendering myself to X I move from one of its theaters of despair to another. Delivered up to X I am incapacitated for the observation of trees, cafe habitués, streets—all the official raw material whence my vocation, ostensibly at war with the descent into X, strengthens its sinews. I loathe myself cutting myself off from all this precious raw material. All down my peregrinations I can feel myself fighting in vain the disorder and deprivation suppurating from the wound of my thralldom. I am plunging

5

far, further and further, from the legitimate site of acquisition. All is lost. Paris has never seemed darker, less yielding. Then a thought comes, not far from the Place Clichy. The thought tells me though I feel myself fighting against the ostensible chaos induced by thralldom to X I refuse to feel myself fighting, through X, via X, as X, armed with X, suffused with X, against the rigidly imprisoning edicts designating what is and what is not legitimate fodder for the vocation,—for being, in other words, since it is only through the vocation that I am at all—which I construe as emanating without pause from its every nook and cranny. This thought, in addition to being a bona fide acquisition to be opposed to the obliteration waiting at every crossroads, also awakens me to the possibility that in its way X embodies a fight, my fight, to be. It might be more than an embodied negativity, a fanged void which has somehow managed to usurp the ground of my real being. Yet as anything but an embodied negativity can it be useful to me, that is to say could it serve as a pretext for thought, thoughts. After all, a thought came, not far from the Place Clichy, on the wings only of a conspicuously failed fusion with X as a defiance of withered injunctions, received ideas.

And why has the thought come. Why did the thought come then. What was the meaning—what is the meaning—of a thought . . . coming. Has the thought been sent to mask a painful truth (that X is and will always remain incompatible with the vocation's legitimate cravings) or as the only possible instrument for unrolling for my inspection an opposite equally painful truth. This quandary has itself the makings of a thought, that is to say an acquisition.

Just before I redescend I tell myself thoughts will be impossible once I feel myself at one with X. Thoughts will exit only from the seams of a failed coincidence between me and X.

Toward the middle of the afternoon I am approaching a saturation point. But I can never be sure when I might redescend in blind defiance of my own satiation. I am never sure how long I will be able to tolerate the sunlight. I have a beer, standing up at the counter, in a crowded cafe on the Place Clichy and then, for no apparent reason, begin a descent of the Rue Clichy, buying and devouring en route two green apples from a small grocery less from hunger than as a tentative affirmation of renewed connectedness with the real world, the clean busy world beyond X. I devour them also to be rid of them as quickly as possible, for once purchased they are immediately impedimenta on the way to, on the way to, on the way back to X.

Reaching the *grands boulevards* I decide to eat in a self-service. Only when I am well into the meal do I realize how deeply Parisian self-services depress me. Outside it is greyer than it has been all day, I am abundantly overcome with fear of loved ones' loss. I believe that by entering a self-service I will be spared the humiliating confrontations inseparable from sitting down in even the lowliest bistro. But here, among these others equally dispossessed, humiliation has been supplanted by overwhelming grief and fear rendered all the more overwhelming because unmitigated by prickingly abject collision with restaurant chessmen. The sky becomes too grey. I surrender to X. Yet once surrendered I feel that I have only to wrench myself free of its coils to be spared every conceivable form of torment. I wait. The thought comes: Descent into X as a flight from torment is immediately transformed, descent achieved, into an impediment on the way back to clean and manly confrontation of those torments, which confrontation viewed wishfully, wistfully, from the depths of X is indistinguishable from nothing less than torment's end. The thought continues: It is the evasion of torment (excruciated separatedness from loved ones, from all of being) in the depths of X that is equivalent to, induces, torment. When viewed from the vantage of an impeding X separation is no longer characterizable as unappeasable torment. Saddled with the supplementary anguish induced in surrender to X I find myself saddled concomitantly with nostalgia for the torment, all those anguishes, masked behind lopsided allegiance to X, to the grammar of X. The virulence of these anguishes are not inherent: It stems from the virulence of X's obstruction of manly confrontation.

I run out into the Boulevard St.-Denis. I find myself there where the pavement rises high above the thoroughfare. The next morning I again take breakfast in the hotel. Walking all down the Boulevard de Latour-Maubourg I am invigorated, ecstatic over the renewal of an intimate relation with my favorite city, at the height of summer already on the verge of autumn's fragrant chill. I am far from the craving to re-immerse myself in X. My slate is wiped clean. Purity runs through me all the way down to my bowels. But will this rehabilitatedness last, will I be able to wander in neighborhoods far from my signposts, the theater of my degradation. As a good tourist will I be able to contend with the upsurge of details that have nothing to do with X. I proceed down the Rue de Rivoli to the *grands boulevards* and upward to the Place de la Republique. Sitting in its park, beside the fountains and the mutilated-looking trees, I examine my map. I am comforted. The clouds overhead are comforting even though they are purposefully massed against the sun's emergence. A thought is imminent. I am about to be rearmed, to acquire an arm. A thought is on the way. A thought is coming. A thought enshrining the connectedness of X to other states of affairs is on its way. I take a deep breath. The thought's imminence allows me to think seriously, detachedly, of X. Is there, after all, so much difference between immersion in X and legitimate activity —what I am doing now, for example, sitting absolutely still and getting my bearings as the vehicles charge past. Reading my map, I begin to accept myself as the site of a skewed compatibility between X and all the legitimate and eminently acceptable activities that need never, X-like, cringe against the incursion of daylight. The thought arrives fully-formed: Turbulent anguish emerges not so much in thralldom to, immersion in, X as from the need to separate, to render it highly distinct and distinguishable from the sunny quotidian's respectable doings. Once again: Not A but B. Once again: Vengeance on straitjacketedness, fixedness, localizedness, in being, in my own particular form of being. The thought jostles me forward: Repressing its memory during those daylight or rare hours of night when I am allowed or forced to commingle with the legitimate particles of my chosen vocation, I merely perpetuate X, nurture its infernal glamor and insure its recrudescence. Insofar as I assimilate it as a legitimate constituent of my being I rob X of some of its virulence. But so legitimated, I wonder, is it still X, does it still partake of the substance of X. That is, so devirulized, does it still qualify as a thought-producing machine. I am not sure, staring at my ragged map in the heart of the Place de la Republique, whether this last query is part of my thought or a reaction against it.

The Quai de Jemappes is almost deserted, except for a tiny fish writhing its last in a net. After noting the footbridges along the canal I turn into a street, the Rue Bichat. It drizzles. When I emerge from my winding foray it is sunny once more. It is even sunnier and warmer in a little park off the Rue Boyer. A child passes through with its grandmother. I am sad but no longer tortured. There is something in this little park which soothes, maternalness intervenes at its most unthreatening.

In a few minutes, by métro, I am steps away from the Luxembourg Gardens. I enter, sit down on an iron chair along one of the many paths. I think back to the dark drizzle infecting the Rue Bichat. With the sun blazing unequivocally now I am for a split second transported far from the site of misery. Tabulating the distance I have come, from drizzle to dazzle, in so short an interval thanks to the efficiency of the underground and the delirious mutability of the skies above, I am catapulted far from my origin in grief, helplessness, excruciated separatedness. The witnessed change from drizzle to dazzle suggests that my present fixedness, stratjacketedness, localizedness in gapless pain, will also change, end. Measuring how far I have come—from the Avenue Gambetta to the Boulevard St.-Michel—I am transported, I am the distance between these two quartiers, more, between two states of being, participating in both and in neither— completely . . . inconceivable, unlocalizable, therefore insusceptible to pain. The state, or rather the statelessness, does not last. All of a sudden I am prey to another incarnation of despair. Once again I find myself out on a limb without benefit of the tightrope that lured initially. Somehow the contrast between drizzle and luminosity, at first so bracing, so delightful, is now boding ill. The contrast is now simply a . . . detail. I look around. Trees, playgrounds, tennis courts, *manège*, *pissoirs*, little *lac*, all these details are lovely and ultimately disruptive. I have fallen back to being with a thud, the excruciation out of all proportion to the impact. I continue to look around, to stretch myself out on the rack of details.

I am conscious that I see them now with two successive sights: first of pleasure and second of raging pain that their loveliness should be lavished *now*, under these circumstances. Details exist to torture my solitude, enhance my separatedness, contrast expressly with my penury. Still I go after them. I turn around. Outrageously, a man is sitting on the grass behind a bush eating American fast food. Another detail. Another twist of the knife. Encounter with this detail, with each and every, is a spasm of flight. Perceiving the detail I leap toward it leaping toward me. My anguish is obliterated for I am indistinguishable from the fused leap and a leap (timeless, spaceless) does not undergo, is never susceptible to, pain, my kind of pain. Going to greet the detail expatriates me, blissfully, out of being. But then, but then, colliding with the detail I am reminded of its context which is, always, always, the same context. I am rebounded back to the world, to the context of the world —the world as a totality of details all smelling of the same slogan. Life—details—goes on. I am separated from those I love, I am, they are, every moment prey to annihilation, but life goes on.

Sitting on the bench, at the very heart of the detail circus (a leaf falls), consists in fact of the incessant resurgence and decay of the pulsion to get up and go away, back to X, far from the excruciation induced by the omnipresence of details. Initially, they all strain toward me with the promise of the beginning of the end of pain, of separatedness, but then . . . Sitting on the bench is perpetually smothered flight from the bench. This is what sitting means. This is its concept. The part of me that will, at the drop of a hat, unfurl its allegiance to the vocation's legitimate enrichment, wants to remain, acquiring traditional raw materials—thoughts about trees, paths, ice cream vendors —tourist thoughts, broadened-horizon thoughts. The other part wants to run. Back to X. Away from the reminder that I am separated not only from my loveds but from all of being as a sum of details.

It is dusk. Not only is the air cooler, windier, the park has thinned also. Dusk is . . . exquisite. Then why am I compelled to run from it. Once again I feel how X pulls me away from a suitable field for the expanding exercise of "vocational skills" but not how X, single-handedly, saves me from the excruciation latent in even the most peripheral immersion in that field's— dusk's—warm bath of crystalline beauty. Dusk is not kind to the solitary.

I run toward the métro on the Boulevard Raspail. The tower in the middle distance buoys me up. It is exhilarating to be, once again, within minutes, on the other side of Paris. These shifts breed a kind of defiance, a sense of having shamelessly colluded against all others—the very laws of life—all who must condemn me for the feverish ignominy of my flight. As I am about to reach the glass doors just below street level saying, Excuse me, I hurry past someone who threatens to swerve into my path. I catch my tone. It is not, surprisingly, the tone of one run ragged by obsession. No, it is not the tone of one run ragged by obsession, it is much more .. much more ... Once again, a thought is on its way, I am propelled forward by what I am about to acquire. No, it is not the tone of. .. it is much more the tone of. , not A but B. It is much more the tone of one who, with quiet heroism shelving his own preoccupations, hurries surefooted to the site of another's crying need. My tone is much more that of one about to intervene on behalf of what has absolutely no connection to his own being, his own picayune well-being. For a moment it is no longer I surrendered to X, to the protocol, to the grammar, of X, I am merely taking the part of one so surrendered. But without the least trace of condescension or reproach.

Vocational

It is not easy describing first sentiments embarking on my new career. All was joy, pleasurable panic in anticipation of untried sensations and sentiments. My co-workers showed themselves almost overly fond of me and of the panic-ridden exertions they presumed, presumably, I would ultimately outgrow.

At first, addicted to the most unswerving scrupulosity didn't I have even the slightest sense that all this busyness was simply paving the way toward an inevitable, a plausible, disillusionment. I see now that disillusionment was all along the true vocation, the unassailable vantage, on any and every version of vocational striving.

For a long time I believed honestly enough in every task eagerly executed, every supplementary chore gratefully assumed. Most of all I believed in my gentle smooth-tongued braying competent fondness for the clients shuttled my way. It was inconceivable that I should not love 'them, love their ills; not consecrate myself to the grim pursuit of their resuscitation; not do all I could to let a little of the sunlight into the maze thwarting my every thrust on their behalf.

I succeeded very fast in winning the contempt of the higher-ups. Their uneasiness at my ungainly alacrity was manifested all too glibly as disdainful tolerance. It was easy to neglect that disdain because my incessant . . . scurrying had completely deranged my prior conception of myself. More than a heroic figure I had become exquisitely poised, able to contend expertly with the supplicating convergence of all bleary eyes. What was responsible then for the ever mounting feelings of rage, of hatred, toward faces and figures that, only a short time before, had been capable of inspiring an exclusively gentle and unflagging assiduity in the service of a singlehanded resurrection of the recumbent civic virtues. All of a sudden I was completely depopulated of all interest in my vocation and dedicated instead to a kind of sub-vocation, virulently unforeseen and infinitely ductile ramification of the sire it threatened in no time at all to render fatuous, obsolete.

Why could I no longer tolerate the ravaged gazes. Why was all that concentrated helplessness suddenly being undergone as nothing more than . . . bad form. It would be too easy to say that too many encounters with the arrogant ineptitude of the higher-ups had succeeded finally in marring the blazoning surface of a previously flawless accessibility to cries and crises. I myself knew I had begun hating them long before the wizened tree of experience bid me pluck its fruit. You could say that disillusion-ment, my particular initiation into the protocol of disillusionment, moved from the very start at a clip briskly out of all proportion to the glamorous instances that might be held accountable for its enlargement. might be said to have legitimated it. You could say that disillusionment had, from the very start, been dedicated to tearing itself free of legitimating instances, accessibly plausible provocation. Yes, from the very start, disillusionment had made it clear, if only I had taken the trouble to lend an ear, that it intended to lead a life, a life largely charmed, of its own and where stalwart repudiation of vulgar connectedness to causative occasions must figure prominently.

Disillusionment had been there from the very beginning, prior to the very beginning. Not a germ of disillusionment but disillusionment fully formed. Hadn't I known in advance of all falls to specific vocation that no vocation would serve, willingly at least, as conduit toward the dazzling fulfillment of unavowed deepest aspirations. It is no wonder, then, that scrupulosity was.

for one of my ilk, synonymous with martyrdom. What for the others was an everyday matter of getting the job done in order to pay the rent, the electricity bill and the grocer became for me an extravagantly gratuitous flight into self-laceration. Of course I too was working to feed the breakfast table but it was somehow extremely easy to bracket those contingencies and pretend—no proclaim—that I toiled for no earthly reason whatsoever. From time to time there were sobering reminders of governing contingencies. The reminders, in an exasperatingly discreet undertone, whispered that I simply worked to . . . be. How inform these reminders that I had absolutely no desire to be as I observed my co-workers condemned to be. Riding pillion on the wings of disillusionment how make it generally known—but did I want that—that I was out for stakes higher than a paltry parcel of being. What were all those fluttery motions of martyrredness but a way of alerting my spectators to an, as yet, tenuous relation to another realm, different from theirs, in which I was very much on the verge of staking a claim yet about whose dimensions nothing, positively nothing, could be said. There was one among them—actually he was a bit higher-up—who had no tolerance whatsoever for the unfolding of my plight. His target was, from the very first, the boundlessly raging hatred whose ceaseless ebullition was poorly squelched beneath the lid of a hunger to oblige. One day he said, "Why do you stick around." "I'm here so that, at the appropriate moment, I can be located." "Rescued?" he sneered. "Located." "Located then." I winced at his use of this word. Even though he was using the same word I underwent his utterance as a correction. Taking me roughly by the arm he led me into a shadowy and chilly alcove, far from the huddled and helpless few who remained to be seen. "So, you are expecting your negligence, your carelessness, your incessant evasion of your duty, to end up provoking the notice— that is to say, the intercession—of some other." "I am scrupulous," I replied. "You are scrupulous," he said. He hadn't moved a muscle but his inflection made it appear as if he had raised his eyebrows. "I am scrupulous. Nor have I ever been anything but scrupulous." My inflection I had managed to depopulate of all quavering. "What amazes me," he began, looking deeply at the mobile shadows on the low bulbless ceiling, "is how you are able to go on insisting on your scrupulosity dead in the face, that is, of all the evidence." Unflinching I murmured, "Evidence." "You insist on your scrupulosity knowing full well that you are rarely scrupulous and when you choose to be scrupulous what you call scrupulousness is nothing more than a mindless flutter, a vastly fleeting fellow-feeling. Yet knowing this as well as I do you never feel that you are lying or if you know that you are lying that your lying in any way detracts from the need to go on lying on behalf presumably of some preponderating countervailing truth. You insist on your scrupulosity despite all the evidence that pinpoints its nonexistence. You cast that evidence aside as so much flotsam obstructing our global, our monumental, vantage on things as they are, as they might be, as they ought to be and therefore, somewhere—in some plane—the plane in which you are no longer a liar—are. That plane is no doubt favored with the conspicuous absence of those degrading exigencies enjoining, for purposes of brute survival, the abnegation of a continuous exercise of your talent for scrupulosity." "I've been scrupulous," I intoned. "Yes, you've been scrupulous if scrupulosity can in some way be stretched to comprise an intermittent fidelity to routine for the purpose of self-localization, easy accessibility lest the emissarial artisans of a more exalted destiny miss you once they decide to descend en masse. You stay here so the messengers will know where to locate you." I wanted to protest but before opening my mouth I realized that this . . . diagnosis was pretty much what I had hinted at before. It was far more accurate even than paraphrase. Then why did I want to leap forth and strangle my interlocutor as if he had said something strangely, injuringly, new. Saying the very same thing was somehow a verdict on my failure to, conclusively, say. My saying was rendered, retroactively, an evasion by the hardly exceptional precision of his repetition. He had said nothing new and yet I felt rebuked, as if coerced into looking an eluded unpleasantness dead straight in the eye. "You don't believe in what you do here. You simply persist. It's no vocation. You know what it is?" I did not move, did not breathe. "A receptacle for the passage of time. Brute duration flowing inevitably toward what you have to construe—or else you'd go mad with rage—as apotheosis. Not that apotheosis is to be considered the culmination of your doings here. Oh no, oh no. For all that slumbers toward apotheosis slumbers from a completely different direction." "And what is doing the slumbering?" "Some subterranean, quasi-recondite activity—like picking your nose—completely indecipherable, completely gratuitous yet perversely committed to inserting itself into the nonconverging sequence of endeavors that make men men. No, better yet, apotheosis will be the fruit of no activity, no doing whatsoever. Apotheosis will be the culmination of nothing converging on nothing. Maybe for somebody of your ilk the only apotheosis worth undergoing—the only apotheosis worth its salt—is the kind that is reward for and culmination of no given, no fixed and localizable doing. Your apotheosis comes, pantingly, at the end of . . . abstention, of having abstained, of having always and forever been on the alert, on the very fringe of being, supremely dedicated to the excruciation induced by gapless vigilance over time passing. Under these circumstances, apotheosis is the logical outcome and endpoint of surrender to brute duration: its flow, its sludge. Unmitigated surrender. Apotheosis is, under these circumstances—but what are these circumstances precisely—the only rightful, the only conceivable, reparation for unswerving refusal to be enticed away, distracted. You have alighted among us here as a way of being absent from another site." "Another site." "The site of your destiny's consummation. Here you keep yourself—you are kept—out of the way of whoever or whatever, artisanally, is fashioning an appropriate reward. Absence is purity. Unheard, unseen, you no longer emit a terrible stench that can only obstruct the progress of those artisans. Reconsituted into one flawlessly pure you find yourself become worthy at last—worthier and worthier—of the royal robes they must be stitching together without respite so as to be in time for the qualifying ceremonies." I did not know how to answer. Was it possible to conceive of an answer. Wasn't this type of driving oration designed especially to render the notion of an answer obsolete. The remark about my stench hurt especially. I tried to edge away. I tried to dive back into a pocket of clients. Back at my post I found a young lady waiting. Coming up to the counter she told me she had not come for herself. Or rather she had come looking for a job. "I need a job. I need work." She began to weep. Seeing her weeping, and hoping, perhaps, that my brash incompetence was the cause, the sub-chief was beside me in seconds flat. Overcome—or so it suddenly seemed to me—by her good fortune in being delivered up to an audience of more than one she said, "I'm dying of grief. Walking the streets I find myself hoping only for a quick annihilation. Nothing to hope for, to look forward to. And nothing to distract, nothing in the landscape to call my own. Every detail is absorbed—sucked—back into the whole before I can appropriate it. Every detail belongs to the whole and the whole is stationed against me. So that there is nothing to choose in that whole, no this instead of that. There is nothing but the whole." "All this because you don't have a job," I said, hoping to annul the sub-chief's involvement. She looked at me, incredulous, as incredulous at my question as I at her state of mind. "I know people who have reacted even more gruesomely." She turned to my former interlocutor as if for corroboration. He nodded slightly. I caught the nod. He flinched, not having wanted me to see it. "What is it about the landscape that makes it . . . unsatisfactory?" he queried, trying to show—me, presumably—that he was absolutely disinterested. "It isn't

18

unsatisfactory in any single detail. When you've reached the point I've reached the landscape is never unsatisfactory in any single detail." Looking pointedly at the space between us, she said, "To find the landscape unsatisfactory in this or that single detail is a luxury of lesser minds." Then realizing that she must not antagonize us—him—she added in a softer tone and one more in keeping with her self-assigned status of symptomed being, "I'm somehow beyond the stage of its being a question of liking this tree instead of that. In my condition, the whole—the global landscape—is unsatisfactory. Perhaps precisely because there is no way to, no motive for, choosing one detail over another. In relation to this whole, the question of choice—election —is inconceivable. And there is, of course, no question of alternative wholes. There is only this, this whole, this monolith, this fisheye bringing home without surcease, without benefit of euphemism, the fact that I don't bring home the bacon." "What can we do?" I said, making use of the standard question broached by staff to clients. "Rescue me from suicide, give me a job. Let me work." Before either of us could respond she added, "The grief is overwhelming." But before I could speak my thought, even think it, my sub-chief and interlocutor, whose name was Big Bob, was already speaking, boldly, even rudely, "Your grief." Long, long pause. "Your grief can't be all that great, little lady. I mean, after all, you've managed to get dressed, grab a cup of coffee, make your way over here to this relatively out of the way place." She thought a moment. "You're right. It's always like that. Just when it seems I will be unable to endure the pain one minute longer I find myself lifting a pencil or stopping to button my coat or running to catch the K-595 bus. But don't think I'm not appalled, as appalled as you, by the sudden spasm of robustness, grief-defiance. How can I pretend to be grieving when all of my exertions are so much a clear and callous repudiation of the grief. But as a sub-chief of staff I hope you are aware of the paradox latent here." Big Bob looked up. Slightly intimidated, I

19

thought. "The greater my grief becomes the greater the sense of a dissimulation. The greater my sense of overwhelming misery the greater that of somehow betraying the misery at every turn since—so high are the standards I set for myself as one overwhelmed by, committed to, grief—I can still pick up a pencil, breathe, gnash my teeth. In other words, if I were truly wedded to grief I would be incapable of all that, gesturally, puts the seal on my condition as that of one who grieves." "So what have you learned from the grief," Big Bob said casually, impatiently. He was trying to show that it was of absolutely no importance to him to have missed the paradox. She winced—I saw her wince. Although he had merely just repeated her word she was clearly undone. It was as if somebody, an ill-intentioned bystander, had—through persistently venomous overhearing—stumbled on the correct word for her predicament. All of a sudden. Out of the blue. She drew back. She underwent the barest repetition as an accusation. "Sometimes I come out of the grief—for there are times when I do come out of it—believing that I have learned, am inured. It is as if I am no longer hoping. Until that moment, that is, when I find myself hoping once more and pretty much in the old way. Which only leads me to believe what I have always known deep down—namely that grief never enlightens but merely stands in as a kind of placeholding penance necessary if—narcotizing until—the true target of hope rises in the east. Grief allows me to undergo—" 'Brute duration," I murmured. She stared. "I always believe that the vastness of my grief signals the end of lacerating hope until I wake up one fine day finding myself prey once more to the old craving. So I think it is safe to say—" she smiled, taking us both in as if we might be future constituents, "—that grief does not so much cure as exacerbate the old hopeful craving. One secretly expects some kind of recompense for all the strenuous undistracted incubation of brute duration's bruteness." "Is the job your recompense," said Big Bob. "No, wanting a job signifies that I am alert to the

20

danger of the old hopeful craving's recrudescence. I want to fight against it. I want to repudiate it." "Well," he finally said. "I don't see that it can do much harm if you settle down here among us folks." He tried to drain his physiognomy of all emotion but it was clear, at least to me, that he was very much moved by the pleasure he was giving

Within a very short interval she had succeeded in appropriating many—most—of my duties, thereby allowing me to spend more and more time out in the parking lot adjacent to the tenement. This modification meant that I could consecrate myself almost totally—globally—to . . . the anticipation of my reward. With her on the scene I was in the position at last of never having to turn my face from time passing. I was ecstatic until the day came when she was obliged to take me aside—I had come back to get my hat and satchel on the way to lunch—and whisper diffidently, "When you spoke to that old lady over there—"—she did not have to point, it was the only female in the bunch that day—, "you forgot to obtain her identification number or to give her one." She ended quickly but not incoherently as if trying to get this unpleasantness over with as soon as possible—to surmount, specifically, as the most miasmic temptation of all, surrender to a simulated casualness and false flat fellow-feeling. All the same I felt attacked, attacked at the core of my very being. Her decorous reprimand pinpointed a taint that disqualified for any further pursuit of my aims. So tainted—by ineptitude, by negligence—I was necessarily uprooted from fixity, from the site whence rescue was anticipated. Now I was nowhere to be found, localizable nowhere because no longer wedded to routine, or rather to an unexceptionable performance of that routine. Being suddenly unlocalizable frightened me. And she was responsible. Now the artisans would never come. Now they would never know how to find and finding absolve me, in time, that is, to qualify for the apotheosizing ceremonies. I wanted to run out to the parking lot. There the artisans of my destiny must always know me. "He

21

told me . . . " I stammered. "I told you?" she replied immediately
and there was rage in her tone. This betrayal of rage infuriated
me for all along we had been proceeding as if the merest expression
of rage was colossal bad form, Rage, shrillness, exasperation—these
were the prerogative of the petty higher-ups. Only trivial souls
succumbed to the expenditure of large-scale emotion on such
small-scale doings. I sensed that the memory of this moment-this
split second during which her rage had cornered me—would be
excruciating, almost impossible. "No, he told me. He told me
never to give or to obtain a number during a first encounter. . . "
I knew he had never quite said this but I had to fight back, or
rather I had to have a placement from which to fight back,
blindly. Repudiating her imputation of a taint I only made
myself more ridiculous, however. In defending myself what was
I doing but indicating how much in thrall I was to the blabbering
directives of some other.
I wasn't sure whether it was ineptitude itself—the absolute
value of the ineptitude—or rather my uncertainty about what
had caused her to bring it to my attention now—which most
contorted my precarious equilibrium. Had her exasperation simply
caught her off guard or had she been planning all along to catch
me in her net . . . If so then an invalidating sourness was already
cast over all our previous camaraderie. It was as if she had
finally stumbled on her chance to repudiate our alliedness, to
humiliate me for fixing her in my site, the site of an estrangement
from all that went on and did not go on around us. It was as if,
for all our easy raillery, regarding helpless clients, chiefs and sub-
chiefs, it had finally dawned on her that such raillery, such
savage mockery, was in fact a fixative, a straitjacket. Identified
with me, identified with the wisecracks that proliferated in my
vicinity, she would have had to come to terms with herself as a
type, a stock character, a definable diagnosable entity. She
refused. I tried to be casual, to hold up my head, to make the tail
between my legs as inconspicuous as possible.

From then on I tried to show a little more steadfastness, a little more competence. But word was out. In the midst of the most gruesome details of case histories, every client—never mind the succession of pitiless evictions, the bloody street battles, the mounting hypophyseal tumors—found a foothold whence to contemplate the preposterousness of my dedication, the hilarious futility of my efforts—paroxysmal, at best—to intercede. No matter how dire their straits my fatuity managed always to become the central event, the key feature. It is no wonder that, to escape all this, I spent more and more time in the parking lot. Letting her run the show indoors it was there that brute duration passed me by most conspicuously. It was there I did time most conspicuously. Did time for the benefit of the artisans.

One day as I was going back to get my coat and hat and to suffer the reprimand of the day—I remember it as if it was yesterday, the surrounding skyscrapers looked as if they had swum, windowless, into the azure at that very moment—I observed the subchief advancing upon me. I tried to turn on my heel. In vain. I tried to gather strength telling myself that the sun was beating down as mercilessly on his head as on my own. His had more bald patches. "Ho, ho," he cried, in an ingratiating tone wide enough to absorb all my lapses, all my misgivings, "no need to run." Never had he seemed so much to deserve the title, subchief, and in the bureau of client orientations and approvals. It occurred to me he might have come to deliver her reprimand. Finding herself too busy to scold she had decided to delegate to her immediate superior the onerous—Was that her, in fact, standing on high heels in the lobby. "I know I should be back in there, collecting identification cards—" I stammered. "But there are moments when—" "When one hates them. Hates it. I know." Was he trying, through a kind of virile flattery, to fatten me up for the inquisitorial kill. If he was sincere his efforts to fraternize revealed an even greater gap between us than I had imagined. Wasn't he implying that sporadically I hated my charges, our clients, only because sporadically I found myself confronted with the vast of my own impotence, that is to say finitude. Clearly—if he was sincere—he did not see that I hardly cared if these soon-to-be-slaughtered billions lived or died. Clearly he did not see that to one of my tastes the misery of others—these others—was at best and nothing more than an impediment, an obstruction, on the way to, on the way, to, to . . . The only edification to be derived from their deformities—flagrantly paraded—was that clearly, clearly, my fate could always worsen and that up to now—whatever my symptoms—I had merely grazed the virulent wing of contingency. I had by no means achieved the peak of misfortune—my deformities could, or so it seemed, be turned on and off at will. Whereas they . . . I was suddenly overcome with a new access of rage against the clients. Decked out in all the gaudy autumn coloring of their brands of adversity they might at this very moment be distracting my artisans from their true work. "I should go back," I said. "Stop worrying about what's happening in there." "But I'm neglecting—" "It's not your negligence that disturbs me. In any case, it's a phase, you'll get into shape. Soon. I know it." As I did not seem to be taking much heart from his dicta he increased volume and frequency adding, "It isn't negligence in the usual sense. Let's call it instead a kind of slumbering before the great . . . the invigorating leap." I did not answer. "But what does worry me is your having chosen this little refuge. You don't seem at home." "Where." "Here, in the parking lot." I started to move toward the lobby. "You seem to be trembling and your tremor is spreading to everything." "Stop trying to make me feel . . tainted," I cried. "My tremor may try to spread to everything but nothing is affected, everything surrounding me—and not just the skyscrapers over there—is simply too lofty to bother about ejecting me firmly and permanently from its premises Anyway. They're used to my kind being plagueyly out of touch with what should be—and under normal circumstances is—capable of inducing and sustaining well-being in every single pore. Clogged or not." Opening the door of his car he shouted, "I'm not interested in your kind. I'm interested in you." I did not answer. "Get in," he added. When I was seated in the back and just as the car was turning—madly I thought—this way and that to tear itself free of the tarry turf crisscrossed with yellow lines—as my disillusionment had, long before, torn itself free of disillusionment-inducing contingencies—she ran out of the lobby into the parking lot. The car was so positioned that it was very simple for her to open the front door and glide in beside him. As they—as we—drove off she made the silence plausible by breathing deeply—to signify, presumably, fatigue, deep fatigue, but a healthy invigorating fatigue—and touching up spots in her chignon. The vehicle proceeded swiftly, through wrecks and bottlenecks. He stopped in a small shopping mall to buy two or three loaves of peasant bread and a case of imported beer. The several guests already assembled, scrutinizing us both from head to foot, tried nevertheless to outdo each other in desinvolture. At the dinner table seeing me for all practical purposes lost amid all the beams and luminosities of her stout cordiality—her unflinching cordiality—the hostess turned to me and pointing in the direction of the window said, "Mrs. Ruritanie, a physician." Then gently redirecting my glance in the opposite direction—less through gesture than through inflection—to a withered little figure nibbling at a wedge of coffee-colored foul-smelling cheese, she ventured, gingerly, as if her classification might in some way mar the thing classified, "Mr. Mac Dwykers. Lawyer." Here was one then whose slobbering prostration before professionals— whose hunger to formulate and classify—was easily enought arraigned. Should the weary traveller be so inclined. I was about to begin disdaining her but then I realized it was a relief, an authentic relief, to have the landscape so partitioned into doctors, lawyers, and their ilk. If only I too could be assigned a placement, a pair of coordinates on the grid, no matter how lowly—something, simply, to tide me over until the artisans (alate) arrived to carry me off by the scruff. But she did not see her way clear—or my way clear—to so placing me, localizing me. Fresh from her triumphs on the job I expected my co-worker to shine, to become, at the very least, the minion of the Ruritanie. But she seemed even more ill at ease than I. And somehow she did not look as if some—any—placement might relieve the uneasiness. She seemed to be shrinking from the possibility of such a placedness. Just then—just as the slivers of beef were giving way to the slivers of escarole—the host, my sub-chief, rose. "This one has been with us for quite some time." Outside the trees were barely traceable in the ascending—descending?—expanding fog. However, the trellised gate was perceptible, abruptly perceptible, against the milky backdrop. "I have watched him move from client to client but I cannot say he has manifested any real progress." The sub-chief did not miss a single one of my mishaps, a single one of my ineptitudes. But I was mortified less by the terrifying cumulative urgency of the enumeration than by an impression—no less lancinating for being inchoate—that, for all its assiduity, my disillusionment, my despair in disillusionment, my disillusionment in despair, had not moved quite fast enough—fast enough for the hounds of documenting diagnosis tearing at its rear end. My disillusionment was not yet beyond anybody and everybody's self-assured articulation of its structure. My disillusionment was not . . . inconceivable. Inconceivable to remedy, to rehabilitation. My disillusionment was localizable, diagnosable . . . tellable. The story of my disillusionment was its diagnosis, death warrant. And if my disillusionment was susceptible to placement I too was susceptible. I was placed. Localized for all to see. I felt relieved. The sub-chief, recounting my ineptitudes, had placed me. This way the artisans would be able to keep an eye on me all through their labors on my behalf. I breathed deeply. The air tasted refreshingly sour. Every time I looked up my co-worker had her face, embarrassedly, in her

26

plate. The other guests seemed to recoil from her contraction. In contrast, my movements inspired no horror. Long before, apparently, the menace latent in my flesh and bones had been traded in for the juicy deductions to which their contortions gave rise and which the ever observant host had made a point, obligingly, of laying in a heap before them. After his oration—unfolding and folding back on itself—had done with me—or perhaps just before—just before, in any case, the majority of the guests were preparing to attack the dessert—a piebald citadel of sherbet—the good Doctor Ruritanie turned to my co-worker and said, "So how are things going. Having regular staff meetings, getting to understand the functioning of the—" The screams, the unabashed braying, to which this unassuming question gave rise was quickly smothered by the sound of chairs squeakingly pushed back, feet scraping and stomping their way toward the next room. In a minute the room was deserted, except for the two of us and the corpse at her feet. The host returned dragging a white telephone toward a tiny table near the foggy panes. He shrugged sheepishly. "I have no choice," he murmured. Less at his words than at the sound of his voice—a voice—any voice—the knife, her steak knife, fell earthwards, intercepted by the bloody breastbone of the victim, the late Dr. Ruritanie, nee Incarnadine.

Smiling, unperturbed, the hostess entered saying, "It's a good lesson for all of them. They've been getting too carried away. By their titles and all." My co-worker looked up. Her whole being seethed. "If you're going to reproach me—" she began, unseeing. Once the host and hostess had, for their own good, retreated—the telephone earpiece swayed back and forth in the vicinity of the breastbone as if it would mesmerize it—I moved toward the window. I could see nothing. No warming view of a gravel path taking its time about reaching, amid scrapings and dead leaves, the shadow-flecked garage door. We were, she and I, closed in upon ourselves. "Why did the question enrage you so." She did not answer. I repeated the question. Without looking at me she said, "I needed a job. But I never imagined it would come to this." "To this." I cleared my throat and persisted, "Didn't the question show an active interest in your doings." "Up to a point, up to a point," she replied, trying to be calm. Now she had an aim—my enlightenment. "The question showed an interest in my doings as one who is striving . . . acceptably, as one who is . . . placed, fixed, localized. Don't you know, imbecile, that when you are localized at last it is only a step away to annihilation. Sorry." She smiled ruefully then regretted her lapse to diagnosable emotion. She stamped her foot to annul the lapse. "Her question tells me my work has a place in being. But I refuse, do you hear, I refuse to . . . be. For what is to be but to be a speck on the margin of somebody else's consciousness." She picked up the knife, toyed with it, put it neatly aside. "When I was separate, cast-off, without job, without home, without anything to . . . place me, to render me conceivable . . . intelligible . . . diagnosable—then I felt ferocious, fanged, vibrant." I did not remind her of the state in which she had come to us. "And I conceived of my future vocation, work, job, career—careering —in the same way. Yet fused, in mesh, my vocation and I—we seem to cancel each other out. We become an entity that any idiot—" here she nodded in the general direction of the Ruritanie's demise "—can place, assign to some vacant slot in the universe." "Her question obviously opened up a wound." "Yes, yes," she panted. "A wound. A big wound. Or rather the image at the heart of the question—the image that drove the question—opened up a wound." She looked me straight in the eye, as if to impale me on the purity of a revealed truth. As long as she could count on my skepticism she stood a chance of prolonging the life of that truth. "When she asked me that question—" "About the meetings and the staff," I felt obliged to nod. "When she asked me that question I immediately saw myself as she—as her quesiton—as the image at the heart of her question—saw me. Consigned to a little niche of hustle and

28

bustle, drained of all autonomy. A little puppet, playing out her fantasy of what it must be I was put on this bitch of an earth to do. I immediately saw myself as her smug and thoughtless question saw me—going about my business, or rather, going about the business her presumption had so obligingly, so good-humoredly, drummed up for me. I felt—I knew—there was a kind of exhortation in the question. Oh, you mean you didn't hear it. The question insisted that I conform—and at once—no and, ifs or buts about it—to the image slithering at the very heart of the question. Or rather not so much to an image, her image, for she had no real image—her kind is incapable of synthesizing an authentic image—no the question insisted that I conform rather to the dictates of her desire to have done with me as soon as possible—to have done with me, an unknowable, a raving unknowable, before that unknowability, inconceivability, undiagnosability, unlocalizability, succeeded in overpowering and annihilating her. I swear I had no intention of annihilating her. She brought it on herself."

She looked as if she was about to lift the knife again but thought better of the gesture. "Placing me at a meeting—better yet, a staff meeting—she—or rather the question—or rather the image slithering at its heart—seemed to do away with me faster than I—my unknowability—could do away with her. So patently, so loathsomely knowable, from nape to chaps. The bitch wished to place me before I could be known—make myself known." I intervened in her paroxysm of raucous impenitent laughter "Isn't this, however, what is attempted the majority of the time by all inhabitants of the human soup." She clicked away what she took for appalling levity. "How can I ever forgive the image she tried to evoke." "What image." "Busily chatting, holding forth, at a staff meeting, indistinguishable from all other staff meetings now and forever—sharing (wretched word) my experiences among the simpering clientele and at the same time eager for constructive criticism (nauseating phrase) from my grovelling peers." "The image, what's left of it I mean, presents you as busy—as eagerly participating." "In other words, what's wrong with that—what the hell am I beefing about." I did not answer. I felt attacked—as when Big Bob had spoken of my stench. Perceiving that I was offended—and exasperated by this new trespass added to an already considerable list—she adopted a gruff tone. "Yes, the image presented me as busy—busily participating. And at the same time—and consequently—completely oblivious to bystanders as malevolent as the Ruritanie. Sharks eager to seize on and typecast my busyness—bracket, frame, localize it beyond appeal. Chatting, glorying utterly in my newfound status—in other words, busily participating—what am I but a fleck on the margin of her consciousness, in other words anybody's consciousness,—what am I but an echo of myself, pullulating yet never expanding beyond my own fixed contours on her periphery." "But she sees—saw—we all saw—you as active, diligent, exercising a very important role in the organization. Going to meetings, moving upward." "It is precisely the activity she lent me—the activity latent in the image latent in the question she deigned to ask me—that ostensibly self-affirming but in fact notoriously reductive and self-parodying activity—which straitjacketed and continues to straitjacket me. That sequence of activity, of hustle and bustle, of hurdy and gurdy, of chitting and chatting, what does it converge on that sequence but—stasis. What does it wound to but . . . stasis. A stasis in localizability, nameability. One would think that the kind of activity she had the bienveillance to evoke emancipates, permits the eluding of all fixative, all formulation. No. No. No. On the contrary. This activity, this activity stillborn from the very first, secretes its own fixative, its own imprisoning frame, its own bracket. Such activity quickly finds itself collaborating in the erection of its own very visible limits. Her activity—it was never mine—typed, framed, refrigerated me. Worst of all it . . . legitimated me." She turned away in disgust. Either she was appalled by the image lurking at the heart of her tirade or simply despaired of every painting meticulously enough to be absolutely sure that I too was appalled and for all eternity. I tried, disguising (so I thought) an impatience to rejoin my hosts—only they could localize me anew—to look as if I not only understood but commiserated heartily, appalledly. But she seemed to have reached that point where any expression of commiseration, of alliedness, is as excruciating as incomprehension, mockery. What did my commiseration do but render her plight all the more real. It promised no way out.

On my way back to my hosts I looked back. She had picked up the knife and was stabbing Dr. Ruritanie over and over and over again. Kneeling she did not confine her assaults to the vicinity of the breastbone. Only once—and ever so fleetingly—did she look up at me, as if to say: This and this alone offers some possibility of a way out.

Centaur

It was approaching that time when they advise you to rise and prepare for the anti-vigil they call work. The leaves were scattering in preparation, the sky was black: hopeful enough signs of the only sometimes inevitable rift through which the yellow seeps, expanding. The birds sounding in orchards of trash and the not so distant clatter of dishes numbed him to his own stomach rumbling. What a time it chose to strike up a conversation. His eyes were still closed to the comings and goings of those by and large unaware of the rift. When at last he opened them he could only wonder if those were branches he saw or the sky's very own self-induced fissures. He tried to rise and find out.

Under the name Hercules O'Chez he lived at the Crescent, top floor, with a view of the fashionable suburb adjacent to the not quite fashionable suburb forcing him to drink in its not so potable noon and dusk and now dawn thrown in for free. But rise he could not nor could he sink. What he saw before him was a tableau disintegrating. At first he thought it was the curtain. Then he remembered there was no curtain. The play of the boughs, then, for sure. But his nest was far from trees and their wintry smell. The play of the boughs, the play of the boughs, the sound of the phrase was enough to send him back to sleep investing the disquietude he felt he ought to feel with a lining of cloud.

But what were these slashes before his eyes, blue slashes over a green pseudodepth and green slashes over a red—all these colorations running an unreliable shuttle between surface and depth. Was the depth a real abyss into which one might flee or a mere trick of vision. The tableau persisted well past his realization that its professed abyss was as flat as those he carried within, well past entry of the landlady and her clientela, some blood relations, some not. Before he fully understood his situation of the moment—so much akin to his situation of every moment but nevertheless needing to be understood once again and anew according to the rigors of the moment—he found himself defending it all the more warmly for not understanding, for not wanting in the least to understand. He would never understand until he had at last put it all behind him. Flight, then, was the true, the only, vastation. He planned to stand firm with respect to rehabilitation. Mrs. Quiddity surprised him with her quickness. Who said anything about rehabilitation. They surrounded the bed, satisfying themselves with a little mumbling and chirping. He pulled the quilt up higher, in self-defense. Hercules hoped she had not brought him yet another manual. "There is nothing in your head," said Mrs. Quiddity, opening the window a little on the bottom. She said it with a peremptory sadness that took him back many years, to the forbears he never managed to please. Was it advisable, he asked himself fatuously, to have someone like her around all the time, since by embodying the vicissitudes of his failed past she stymied a rehabilitational recreation from scratch. But he couldn't very well expel his own landlady. She was silent with an earnestness he found touching. "How do you know." "Know what." "That there's nothing there."

"Because, my dear boy, you never put yourself in a position to take anything in," piped up her half-brother, the indefatigable Ace. He pondered not so much the glacial accuracy of this thrust as the subjacent hatred that must mainly be responsible. How else account for this spectacular diagnostic acuity from such a dolt. Hercules cleared his throat, thickly padded at this hour with all the accumulated secretions of uneasy sleep, and fastened the long bone of his gaze on the fat throat of the gaudy lodger. "Centaurs," he intoned. "What? what?" chirped Ace's wife, Cat's distant cousin, of Dickensian grotesquerie. She was a veritable parakeet of a woman with no hint on the surface of her tight broiled skin of that prodigious appetite appropriating as its handmaidens the eager thighs that once wrapped around your back or buttocks invite you

34

to plow deeper, deeper, deepest. "Centaurs," he repeated. "Senators?" she shrieked. Why, people like him shouldn't be allowed to cast their vote, as a dutiful constituent of the less than fashionable suburb she was duly outraged at this cavalier taking of the name of their very reverend representative, Congressman Scheissen, in vain. "Not senators, centaurs," he quietly said, and was soothed for suddenly these creatures, detached from the forest floor, were freefloating before his eyes. "I had that idea without ever getting out of bed." "The one stale idea you were born with," said the landlady's old uncle Aliquot, a pensioner by vocation. He was going through the drawers as if in search of those fabulous creatures. Hercules said nothing being unsure of his rights now that over two months' rent was unpaid. Besides, there was nothing in the drawers but socks and condoms. "Breakfast is waiting," said the landlady, not unkindly. "I wasn't born with any ideas," he told the uncle, as much to enlighten as to interrupt his blundering. "I don't have to go out into the street to take something in. I'm taking things in now." "What?" challenged the voluptuary leaning on the radiator. "I'm not aware of everything I take in. They are minute perceptions. They mount. Eventually, suddenly, all those individual wavelets I did not hear have summated to the sound of the surf that I have no choice but to hear." "No surf around here," proclaimed Ace. "We're miles from the river even." "And that's polluted," the pensioner added, definitively flushed with triumph. The landlady disliked a family quarrel. And Hercules was almost one of the family. She would reform him, the son she had never had, and he could be had. "Maybe he's confusing the rustle of the leaves with surf." But it was dead of winter, no leaves, but nobody thought of that. Only the little voluptuary whose name appropriately was Moana warming to the conversation (the radiator had nothing to do with it) as she forgot her private rancor (Hercules had spurned her advances and on more than one occasion so what if from diffidence rather than clearcut revulsion) in the pursuit of what smelled like truth said, "Or maybe he confuses it with the sound of snow tires coming up the drive." It was clear they were all thinking busily of pretexts for his confusion. After thinking yielded

35

no more dividends they turned back without quite recognizing him. They were utterly unseeing, blinded by the dwindling flame of mystery. Ace, the first definitively to have had enough of this arid speculation, sneeringly said, "I suppose your senator was looking at itself in the mirror." Moana moved closer and closer to her husband and paramour, the angle between her thighs widening. And at the same time making it an extension of her vigilance she seemed to recoil from her own motion, fragile, feline. He was reminded of Cat, conspicuously absent, though if present, would probably have sided with her relations, who fed and clothed her. "No, that's a unicorn," said Hercules. He looked away, drowsy and dead, always when he gave way to what could be construed as pedantry. "I saw a tapestry in the Cluny Museum once," he continued, uncontrollable now. "The world traveler!" Ace sneered. "The world traveler!" said Moana, triumphant. "No, that's a unicorn," he repeated, pretending not to hear, soothed by his own reflective and unrancorous tone, "and I haven't been assaulted by the perception of a unicorn yet. But maybe the minute perceptions are mounting in that direction right now. While we're standing around talking." He tried to beguile himself into a guffaw at the thought of such a strenuous incubation in the half-dark, a private ferment that was reason enough to abstain from the landlady's porridge and compote. They shrugged, less from irritation than from a curiosity they did not wish to acknowledge. The pensioner was stretching one of the condoms, his gaze seemed to swing as in a diminutive hammock under a sun of better days. Hercules decided primly that though once young he was now incontrovertibly a ruin and only because he had never taken the time to believe in his own soul, or more precisely, in that soul's blessed venation. Hercules, in placid contradistinction, knew beyond a doubt that his soul was like, no was, a slab of Carrera uniquely veined as a gingko leaf, the slumbering lineaments awaiting merely the proper chisel. "A gingko leaf," he murmured. The phrase soothingly invoked the tree's mast swaying high above all others, metronoming the pedestrian frenzy of its congener oaks and horse chestnuts and sallows sheathed in their long latency.

36

It was true he needed experiences to incise and contour the fissures of his soul and thereby unveil its latent statuary. But he was not ready to move, especially now when naked under the sheets and perfectly capable of subsisting on minute perceptions. Minute perceptions were certainly more palatable than the stewed prunes of which Mrs. Quiddity's compote supreme largely consisted, more edifying than the manuals of rehabilitation that were her only bed-side reading. "Each day I awaken to a void," he said. "And my minute perceptions replenish the void." "Why should there be a void and at your age," pleaded Mrs. Quiddity. "Don't you have a nice room with plenty of old-fashioned sunshine and hearty country breakfasts. And nice people," she added tentatively, looking round at the living proof. The uncle was coughing, Moana was spreading her thighs wider and wider, Ace was staring absently at the condom that lay atop the chipped bureau, its allegiance partitioned between shadow and reflection. At that moment Hercules was replenished less by his minute perceptions that by the proliferating tics of these interlopers. Ace's forefinger, for example, quivered at his side, completely escaping his hulking vigilance. Hercules felt profoundly sorry for him, for the failure of his essence to appropriate its accidents. The company began to file out. The landlady, last to leave, turned back a parting glance heavy with entreaty. Hercules shrugged almost brutally. No stewed prunes today, madam. Alone at last with his thoughts.

Once a sufficient number of minute perceptions had summated he could embark on his real vocation and leave the Crescent forever, with Cat. Unfortunately this life work seemed much less real to him now that it was made to depend on what was ostensibly preparing him for it. Maybe he was not veined at all, maybe there were no congenital fissures pregnant with future incision. Maybe he was just one big fissure, every orifice a wound. Done in once more by his pusillanimity he hobbled downstairs to announce, "Maybe I'll have some stewed prunes." "And I'll bring you one of those manuals that came yesterday," said Mrs. Quiddity, baldly over-

37

joyed. "I'm going to look for a job." Beside herself, "Now you are one of the eligibles," she cried. Now he could court Cat properly. Abandoned by her first husband she was clearly in need of a good provider, a creature as mythical to O'Chez as a centaur to the condom-hungry pensioner. "Now I am one of the illegibles," he muttered under his breath. She didn't catch on. For too long he had smugly considered himself a trenchant footnote to the words of a text comprising all those folk who hurried to their time clocks each morning. Having made his announcement he returned to his room to dress, that is to say, here was another occasion where he could feel himself becoming an object to himself, watching himself, watching every gesture, for how else could he be sure it was already coupled to its inverse. How else could he be sure that if he extended his arm for a tweezers or a bar of soap or a stiff old green sock his hand or his foot or his thigh would be refunded to him. In bed he could wait patiently for the minute perceptions to mount. Now, as he was thrashing about in his own quarters, in and out of his own hindquarters, washing his face, clearing it of its film and stubble, pissing, farting as he pissed, there was no time for perceptions to mount unperceived. He, Hercules, was too busy striving to achieve some kind of penurious mastery over the perceptions that assaulted mounting and very much, excruciatedly, perceived. And every one of these behemoth perceptions seemed important, indispensable even. He tried to make a frantic inventory of each and every. He regained a little of his self-respect telling himself that it was he seeking out these furry beasts; by no means was he waiting for them to spring, passive, sullen, unresigned. They went on, these gross perceptions, assaulting, almost belching forth as from a fumarole, oblivious of his face-saving stratagems. Everything suddenly mattered, once he was out of bed, yet in a way he did not quite understand. The hairs of the toothbrush, the hairs on the rim of the toilet bowl, the smell of extinguished matches recruited to subdue the smell of shit, the shadow of the palsied twigs beyond the back garden gate on the sooty rim of the bathtub—he could hardly assimilate these messages fast enough though he was by no means sure of what assimilation consisted and toward what life work he was assimilating so frantically. He closed his eyes and counted till ten. Mrs. Quiddity was calling. Maybe Cat would be at the kitchen table, peeling her matutinal orange, proudly and coquettishly setting aside the hippocampal rind. No time to waste or else he would drown. He watched himself close the bathroom door, watched himself descend the stair, watched, watched, watched, until watcher became more potent, more *viable,* than doer, for watcher, if truth be told, seemed to be watching from far back in time, from the distant past, watching, seeing nothing, dissatisfied with everything.

He couldn't get to the kitchen fast enough. Speaking to Mrs. Quid he could forget about the outside world and all it brought him up of unwanted gross impressions. Such impressions could never mount—summate—exquisitely—subliminally—the way a succession of dancers amounts suddenly to a dazzling configuration of conquered space on a propless stage. These impressions were as singular and gross as the human props among which they—among *whom* they—had no qualms about erupting. He decided to live inside the Quid's words. For the duration of her macerated syllables he would be the syllables, coming thereby to no large harm.

She sat down beside him, watched him eat, first the porridge then the compote gruel, chin in the palm of her hand. Her bleary gaze swam in the hallowed miscellany of the gestures he no longer bothered to scrutinize. "Where will you look?" she asked. Before he could answer—before he could even remember what her question meant—the Aliquot appeared. "Him! You know what I found in his room, don't you," he asked pointedly, his eyes luminous slits of insinuation that completely effaced his not so luminous crow's feet. "This!" holding up the condom as if it was a teabag that had been steeped several times too many. The landlady shrugged, advertising her enlightenment by remarking, "I have a manual that explains that once a man reaches puberty—" For Hercules, her enlightened tone was more ominous than the phenomenon she had been dispatched (by whom?) to elucidate. Must he be required to stir puberty's perilous midnight into his gruel. Weren't the prunes, ginger, and stale nutmeg enough? He wanted out. "Insolent!" Uncle Aliquot muttered to his bowels murmuring unintelligibly. He stopped eating, swallowed a pit, folded his arms before him. Clearly it would have been better not to have gotten up at all. He would have been spared this humiliated auctioneering of his very own viscera to the very first outraged comer with the organs under consideration standing in as auctioneer.

It began to rain. Uncle sat down in the place reserved for the fair Cat, still conspicuously absent. At the sound of drops against the panes they raised their heads. They watched the slow migration toward the sill, each engrossed according to his or her humor. Uncle looked slightly dazed, his dewlaps sagged like breasts. Hercules was seized with the same pity he had felt earlier for Ace's elusive quivering forefinger. From a certain vantage his neighbors were all pitiful, quick to genuflect though their tendons were sore, quick to imbibe the state incense of platitude. "Give me that manual," he said in his silkiest tones to Mrs. Q as he put his hand (the one with the most presentable, the most virile, fingernails) over hers. Neither she nor uncle heard his request. Rain docilized them beyond recognition. Stunned he said calmly, "Why get up." That brought Uncle back to life. "Because you want to succeed, my boy." "Because you'll miss your bus," said a voice from the doorway. It was Cat, come to watch the rain fall. With Cat nearby he suddenly felt more sure of himself and a terror of that surety. She seemed to know what he was thinking at all times. This was a frequent consolation to one in his shoes. Though when he could feel all the minute perceptions he could not feel about to debouch on an authentic perception—a bore after so many wavelets slapping the jetty—then he resented her knowingness for the tinsel it surely was. One thing was surer: the sum of his distance from his thoughts and her distance from those thoughts was always constant. His thoughts never belonged entirely to him or to her—except the wavelet perceptions when finally they summated into a true bore. The bore of course belonged to him, or rather, would necessarily have belonged to him if he had existed still. For the bore annihilated him. "Sit down, Cat," said her mother-in-law. Mrs. Quiddity rose and proceeded to dump more stewed prunes into a dish. Placing them before the seated Cat she left the room. "I'll get the manual." "What manual," Cat asked slyly. "I'm going to look for a job," he told her. She laughed, its hemorrhage clotted with a few expressions of good luck. "What line of work?" she asked through the laughter. For a moment he felt he would be impaled on the spear of her gaze. But when the moment passed the spear had been converted into the most delicate of tightropes over which the two of them, he *and* she, were precariously perched. His silence had done her in. Mrs. Quiddity returned with the manual. Cat edged up behind him as he leafed through the photographs too quickly to take much note of a scanty text that blessed the first nocturnal emissions that come without warning to the stripling writhing under the sheets, the first hairs sprouting in the damp armpit and under the flat and supple navel. Uncle elbowed him and said, "Get going, my boy. Rent's got to be paid. Get going." Hercules pushed the dish of pits away and walked to the window to stare at the raindrops made to swerve in their migration by a wincing pane. Cat followed him. Mrs. Q was hovering in the middle distance. Moana entered and begged them all to speak a little more softly: Ace was trying to get some sleep after a strenuous night. Hercules tried to imagine his torso locked in the vise of those thighs. But Moana was gone before his sketch could be verified against her outlines. "What ever happened—to make you turn out this way?" Cat said. The landlady and the uncle were staring, as if Cat spoke for them all, even the absent Moana and Ace. Hercules groped to answer. Only he underwent the same blighted receptivity of upstairs in the bathroom a short time before:The light bulb, the formica stained

41

with orange peel, the knife in the sink to which breadcrumbs clung as if for dear life:These gross impressions were assaulting beyond appeal. No use pretending to have invoked them as a way of testing a superfetatory mastery over being and its indices. But he had to find a place for them. They were crucial, more crucial than the responding phrase he was seeking and the job he was avoiding. "Try, try to remember," Mrs. Q pleaded. She stretched out her arms toward him, evidently following to the letter the instructions of some other manual, meant only for her studious strained perusal. Cat too stretched out her arms and in ironical and ferocious mimicry of her mother-in-law's anguished entreaty whispered, "Try to dismember." For some reason Uncle bristled and said, as if he could restrain himself no longer, "Would you please step aside. I can't see the raindrops." Hercules did better than step aside. He moved toward the hall closet where his only raincoat, without epaulets, without belt, hung. Mrs. Q dropped her arms in disgust and disappointment that this potentially fine young man would not assist in his own rehabilitation. Aliquot was now sitting serenely at the kitchen table reading the raindrops descending with his lips. They were beautifully formed, neither too thin nor too thick. Hercules stood at the door and thought about the rain awaiting him. Vaguely he hoped Cat would follow him. But she did not follow. When he looked back into the kitchen she was gone. Out the window, perhaps: after all, she was a cat. Holding his raincoat before him by the tiny frayed collar loop he took note of the little of his wrist that protruded from his starched whitish shirt. Tiny hairs followed veins a tiny distance up the backside of his palm and then gave up. Veins climbed onward toward knuckles alone. The wrist was undeniably his. Wrist had been spared the incision, the joyless probing, of his landlady, and worse—yes worse, far worse—the pointless mockery of the fair Cat. Wrist had escaped unscathed and so he had every right to escape unscathed into wrist. Wrist seemed to assure him that whatever the gesture expended he would not lose possession of those accessories, body and soul, recruited to the

42

expenditure. For every gesture that went out there would be a gesture that brought him back, to himself, fully refunded, coincided with the Herculean core.

At this very moment, in his skull, expanding and contracting like a bellows, a torrent overcame him, the most lashing downpour he had ever known, mythic as a centaur's prancing, impish, and tenacious lust. The raindrops he hadn't really noticed as they deserved—he saw it now!—to be noticed had mounted into this torrent, this overflow. He was bathed beyond rehabilitation, at least insofar as rehabilitation could be reduced to the fleering prying and anxious probing of a Mrs. Q and/or her daughter-in-law. He heard, as the torrent subsided, Moana moaning above, in anticipation, no doubt, of the night. He saluted Moana and her moans, worth all the manuals in kitchendom. Let all the others raise their collective eyebrow, their great bat's wing italicizing his sudden burst of surety into some hapless shred from a case history. The flood had subsided. He took his last look at the kitchen's interior. The Uncle was still reading the raindrops, Mrs. Q was now counting the pits, Cat was still nowhere to be seen.

Riding the back of the torrent, in the way unicorns are reputed to, he advanced on the street

43

Corridor

The first time they were at the end of the corridor. It was less their infirmity which repelled than the reluctance to catalogue its symptoms. As they approached they were as if, so violent became their spasms of laughter, riddled with bullets. Some of the staff had just come and gone to confirm the diagnosis. But did they know that on the basis of new symptoms richly elicited by their presence the clinical entity had been irretrievable altered.

There were two I especially wanted to assist in their progress toward. Fortunio and Benedictus, or Forty and Ben. I began with silence, a silence that, so I flattered myself, was more far more than the absence of words, had nothing to do with the absence of words. I watched as the presence of the silence induced changes for which they would most probably have had to wait years and then in vain. They did not move much but to the few gestures bred, compressed and rendered luminous against the grain of bare walls I attributed more than the keenest daring, nothing less than the annulment of a lifetime's caution. I found myself wanting nevertheless to cry out, Why don't you move. Why don't you play out your infirmity. Let's get on with it, boys. But then I remembered that I was meeting with them at the end of the tether of a day's labor. Their eyes, bloodshot and at once supplicant and accusing, were plumbs ineluctably dipped toward night's soundless sea. I looked into those eyes and thought—But enough of me. This is their story, that of two weary men who, though pursued relentlessly by loquacious demons, seek a decent life amid the usual sooty perils, the obligatorily unprepossessing temptations.

In short, they were clouds on the horizon of my peace, as I on theirs. Why am I here, Forty asked. I looked around the room, pretended to be conscious of its denudation for the very first time. I'm a stranger here myself. I'm as appalled as you are, my movement seemed to say. Ben looked around too either because my disorientation was infectious or because he too wanted to become a stranger to the ambience with which he had too quickly made his peace. What could such adaptability be good for except marring the purity of his specimen. Ben suddenly said (abruptly discontinuing his pan), Why are you here. To bemoaning his pathos-laden estrangement from his official predicament he preferred tampering with that of another, yanking it into the glare of his tactlessness. I turned to the inflamed pane (it was dusk), the bricks of the institution were positively apoplectic. Then I turned away. Then back I turned. But this second time I was no longer hungry for novelty. This second time I was pointing to my turning, my renewed looking at and through the pane, my reconstituted stalemate in sightless seeing. I struggled to deify the recalcitrance, the depletedness, of my target. In this way I hoped to make them hunger for the pane. I was sure we would all have recourse to the pane at some point(s) in the evening's descent into lucidity. Forty moved into shadow, where his blemishes were capable of amelioration. In shadow, emboldened by shadow, Forty said, What is your room like. Very different, I said. Not so different after all, Ben said. He was right, of course, through the pane same feeble commerce with field and sky.
Tell me about yourself, I said to Ben. Born in a bog, emergence still wildly improbable, Forty ventured. Let him tell it, I said, to the space between the inmates. I always found myself running counter to the direction of childhood, Ben said at last. That is to say, I prompted. That is to say, he mimickingly intoned, childhood was a drapery rendered convulsive by my unflagging efforts to cast it off. Shades of El Greco. And then there was puberty's perilous midnight, his inflection a leer as if he suspected he was pandering to my lowest instincts. The end result, I murmured refusing to make

46

him a present of those instincts, brittle amalgam of curiosity, tittering fear. The end result is retrospect, he said smiling. Every bout with the drapery is now enshrined as a star in retrospect's pollenous firmament. You only remember what you did badly, what, all through the joyless doing, you found yourself forever on the verge of not doing. What was the problem, Ben, I quipped. It was clear he was not ready to yield up the details. Fine with me for I was interested not so much in details as in his—their—reaction to my hunger for details. With Forty fast asleep—the nitty-gritty of rehabilitation clearly bored him—Ben felt free enough to mention Mrs. Fall, a Mrs. Euphemia Fall. Mother? wife? my eyes said. All things to all men, he said, turning toward the pane for a draught of dusk. No, seriously, I persisted. Seriously, he said, I must shield her from your ilk. Though she will never fade even when we are up against the likes of you. The swollen likes of you, he sang. As I looked for my implied paunch impaling his sternum on the dirk of a forefinger he said, Whatever does she see in a mug like me.

I refuse to reminisce, he told me. Reminiscence, in case you aren't aware, is the mother's milk of stasis but hardly of the calm that stasis abjectly craves. He shook his head at what he more than assumed was my smug incomprehension. I was clearly all too like the other staff members who, though all too eager for data, refuse, smiling at the wrong time and always in an unflattering light, its virulence.

I tried not to take his thoughts at face value. I told myself infirmity was localizable not in the thoughts but rather in his distance from these thoughts elaborated as bait, as decoy. Making thoughts of his feelings he annulled those feelings every time. I was sure he was in possession of a lifetime's supply of such thoughts, wrong words in juxtapositions at once crassly calculated and deliriously fortuitous set aside for just those occasions when, as now, outflow was required. I was tempted to say, Your spoken thoughts are a firmament of fortuitous juxtapositions. But I refrained. My job was not to judge, to straightjacket.

As he stood his ground it became clearer and clearer that he was trying to wrest from our combat something more than mere rehabilitation, mere salvation. Any dog, he at last confessed, can be saved. Knowing he was being pumped for details he tormented my greed for gore in the elaboration of thoughts. Let me define those thoughts as quite simply the wrong kind of details. I began to wonder if these thoughts were not, building-block-like, in the service of an edifice in whose labyrinthine pantries and holds I was under no condition to be granted shelter. Out in the stolidly plotted garden he said, You want to know my feelings. But even I don't know them. I know of them. I can never take some discrete interval and say, There I felt pain. Or, there I felt grief. We parried each other's elisions far into the night. Nor did we remain unmoved by dawn's encroachment of ragged bloom, a limpid finery seared by light advancing on stilts. I tried to extract impressions. I was on the verge of begging for words. I had to prepare myself for my colleagues. No small labor to snap back to nimble communion with fellow professionals after a night of short shrift. Yet I knew I was happy to be about to resume my shuttle between inmates and staff. This state of affairs more than any other enabled my to broaden my horizons. But the minute I was out of his sight I knew I must relinquish reconstitution amid the complacency of my peers in the name of another's healing. I followed him at a distance. He seemed hesitant about where to look as he trotted toward a forest of stumps. Where is evasion, his gestures seemed to wonder, in not looking back at the clouds that are tracking me or in not looking deep enough into the black eyes of those advancing to collide with me head-on. Or in making myself the inexhaustibly credulous victim of such a conflict among thought possibilities. I observed that he was carrying chattels under both arms. He carried them as if they were impediments, worthy of jettison. He fell. I . . . felt an emotion. But for the first time words seized and stifled the emotion before it came to birth. The words sketched the possibility of a new emotion toward whose undergoing I struggled as I struggled to keep in step.

The future, my future, was already full of failure to assume the new emotion dictated by the fortuitous juxtaposition of the words, and to expiate the gap between old and new, not unlike that between his clouds before and his clouds behind. We entered a wood. Watching each lanky leg strive in vain to uncouple from the other I felt myself loving all I was, in Ben. I feared being mistaken for Ben, even in that wood remote from all habitation. And yet I found myself suddenly impersonating him, every time I scratched my neck or swung my arms I appropriated his pallor and his rigid envelope sick with suppression of upsurge, outflow. Was he hiding behind a trunk, was he somewhere between trunks. I saw that he was making sure to lose things along the way. I retrieved a comb, a shovel, a pencil. Each footprint was wedded to a residue. I could not help believing that he let things fall in order later to be able to retrieve, to have some reason other than the inexorability of curfew for retracing his steps. When we brushed against each other in a clearing redolent of autumn haze he was bereft of everything. Squandered, he said sodden with pride. He tried to go on. But every time he started he stopped and wanted to begin again.

I wanted to assure him he needn't, this was not a literary enterprise. Over and over he wanted to start from scratch. It was no help telling myself as I witnessed his agony that this kind of thing was by no means unusual among...inmates. As he went about extirpating the irrelevant he very quickly found himself disqualifying every effort, every specimen, as impediment on the way beyond condemnation to all he refused to be. In despair at being unable to surpass what what he smelled always to be a secretion of the same old outworn essence he fled. I watched him go up to his room, deprived of all his odds and ends perhaps he felt a little less coincided with what he shudderingly took himself to be. Silhouetted against the curtain he parcelled out a ration to Forty. Incapable of observing me stealthily from above he descended in a rush. And when I speak, he countered—though I had not, to my knowledge, put forth any sour propositions—how do you know if what I am telling holds any

49

water. I compare with the sample that is you. I compare the sample with the sample that is you, he mimicked. I compare it, I unperturbedly continued, with all you cannot see because you are too busy trying to cancel the effect it produces. It is excruciating for some to coincide with themselves, he pleaded proudly. You will never find a sample to annul the coincidence, I said. The sum of previous samples that is you, I added. And (feeling he was listening attentively, might I say contritely) there is no sample outrageous enough to annul... our kind of connection, our kind of connectedness. Elastic, it accommodates all attempted subversions, and is very quickly strengthened by them.

More of Same

Her story should end at the point where she resolves to remain. By saying, her story should end at the point where she resolves to remain NO MATTER WHAT the persistence of struggle— therefore of story elements—is implied. When her story ends there should be no sense that the story continues, spawning story elements. All that happens must be irreducible to story elements.

Sitting on a bench in the playground out of the blue she told a woman, neither friend, neighbor or acquaintance, "When I don't receive a letter from my mother for a long time, I begin to doubt that he," here she nodded to her son at play in the sandbox, "came from me, from my belly. I have no being if my mother's letter as proof of her continued existence does not awaken me to being." "What about the child's independent being," said the interlocutor, not looking in the direction of the sandbox. "Its being isn't strong enough to reconstitute the being obliterated in my mother's failure, refusal, to write. She writes only when miserable. Rapture and serenity cannot be enunciated without inducing a terrible rage at whoever, now in possession of the proof of that rapturous serenity, is bound soon enough to use it against her." "Use it," queried the listener. "Use it to mitigate the excruciation demanding reparation for itself as greater than all other excruciations." The listener said nothing. The woman went on, "When she does write she thanks me for what she calls my touching fidelity, as if I were an old schoolmate." "Why do you think she minimizes your exertions." "To humiliate me, to demonstrate to me, to the world, that no matter what I do her excruciation remains inaccessible to palliative, to my kind of palliative." To the woman beside her she now added, "Excuse me. I didn't mean to bore you." Surely the apology cost her nothing. It showed that even in the midst of her pain she was, virtuosically, at a distance from that pain. When the woman smiled nervously she realized that these little ostensibly painless shovelfuls into the maw of the awkward moment did more, or rather less, than affirm her virtuosity, did more than just buy her time. They betrayed, chipped away, called attention to her as one frayed. Her child returned, trying to pull her hair;which she had tied that morning into a chignon.

Leaving him with the middle-aged woman who ran a kind of clandestine nursery she went on to the dental clinic. A regular dentist with regular fees was out of the question. She was required to wait like all the others, no longer was she the daughter of Doctor X. She was finding herself through no fault/through every fault of her own in being's steerage. At dinner she spoke of her humiliation, skirting it in such a way as to avoid blaming his plight for her own. Defanging even further she added, "And when you are well-known I will insist that you teach your son to have a sense of worth. So that he never falls into the trap of basking in your glow." It seemed to her that she had very well indemnified him for in any way implying that he was responsible for her humiliation. Her last remark made his celebrity a certainty.

The next day she received a letter. Her mother lamented lengthily the deterioration in health of her son, her daughter's brother. The lingering lesion of humiliation vanished at contact with this lamenting. The lamenting was impregnated with the insinuation that she had somehow failed to act on her brother's behalf. Through some fault of her own her brother was now condemned to this progressive deterioration. Reading on, reading deep into her mother's anguish, the most ubiquitous, the most authentic and at the same time the most calculatedly gratuitous of anguishes, she lost all sense of her own. She lost any remaining grip on an anguish she could oppose to this anguish. Implied in the letter was the fatuousness of her own struggles compared to those of the brother. It was as if her mother was reproaching her for failing to tend to her brother's plight blessed as she undeniably was with eternal exemption from plight. Over the years a kindly willingness to be tormented by the lamenting had induced in mother, father, brothers and sisters, an insatiable thirst for the fulgurations of just the kind of effacedness she felt herself succumbing to at this very moment. It was she who was required to dilate the peevishness of rude dissatisfaction to the dimensions of high tragedy. She was expected to reflect back grievance, rudely tossed, as more than the byproduct of a hemorrhoid or head cold. The slightest deviation from total immersion in the lamenting grievance enraged.

She put the letter aside. In the course of the day she returned to it. Now, far from her mother, far from her mother's anguish, she returns to it, to the torment it induces, from different perspectives. From various vantages of rage and revulsion she bears down on it again and again. Again and again she visits the vicinity of those nodal points whence all might have ramified differently, undergoing thereby without surcease, the excruciation of phantom contact with alternative destinies.

She turned on the television, stationed several feet away from where she had placed the letter, to situate her particular misery, diminishingly, amid the plethora of reported atrocity. Listening to the announcer she underwent the terror of discovering that a lifespan is a mere minutia, too infinitesimal to profit from the glimmer of progress-laden change. "Progress is for those who come after," she said to herself. She went back to the sandbox area and told the same woman about the letter. The woman remarked that she spent an enormous amount of time and energy torturing herself over the indictments disseminated throughout a few sheets of paper. She could barely begin to bemoan the wasteful expenditure sketched by the remark for she was too much enraptured by what was comfortingly suggested of irreproachable martyrdom. She could barely discern what this remark implied so completely did she undergo its reverberations as supremely honorific, as a tribute to a job well done, in this case the job of self-suppression, effacement.

In the every-dwindling shadow of the remark she became, once again, innocent, because annulled. She was terrified, once the shadow faded completely, of being left alone with the substance-lessness of that innocence.

That night she looked especially hard at her husband. Across the dinner table his expression was adequate to any atrocity, the fear, the fatigue, were easily transmutable into disgust and disgust into righteous outrage. When he saw what she saw of his physiognomic refusal to play any role other than that of he who is prepared for the worst he tried to give himself even more strenuously to this refusal to give himself to any situation, to any relation, lest he be compromised, lest he fall into, the intelligibility of spontaneous emotion, recognizable, bracketable, diagnosable emotion. She thought she could detect a frantic plea at the heart of the intransigence. By persisting in his role, his role outside all intelligible roles, wasn't he in the name of some future rehabilitation abstaining from any movement that might mar the lurid outlines of a specimen infirmity pleading frantically for therapeutic intervention. There he sat, mute to the importunity of wife, of child. Piteous figure. As difficult as it was for her, she was coming to realize that her husband's trouble was a separate trouble, that even recruiting all of her ingenuity in making that trouble the outcome of her own glaring defects was bound to fail. Now she was totally out of the picture, his picture, and this terrified.

Once dinner was over and the child in bed he approached her, menacingly, as she half-reclined on the sofa next to the television set. Standing before her, standing above her, he let out, "I did not come home directly yesterday." She swallowed hard against intervention in his difficult presentation. "It was a magnificent evening. You must remember. Sitting above the water I watched without being a part. There were two cyclists beside me. They were part and parcel. They were happy to be part and parcel. Coming back here I know you want me to be part and parcel of . . . something. But I stand back excruciated by the possibility that by participating in that something I am intelligible, doomed to that intelligibility's slow decay." She rose from the sofa, in a frenzy. She opposed him from her full height. He said, "Just before I began talking I felt, Oh what a relief to be able to confess at last. But what I find myself confessing is not what I envisioned as most horrifically in need of confession. What I most need to confess is: When there is in the tone of others, when there is in . . . your tone, the slightest enthusiasm for anything I am overcome with rage."

"So you don't intend to come near me," she said. He did not answer. Anticipating, she tried to perceive his refusal to come near her not as a blighted, an invidious, attack, but rather, and in conformity with his eddying intentions, as a supreme absence of stance resisting all commentary, all accusation in the form of diagnosis. But as soon as she felt safely unable to reproach him—he who had succeeded in resisting all imputation of intention, of fully formed purposefulness—she was immediately overcome with the old affliction of rage and revulsion for this man who refused her, who must destroy everything that arraigned that refusal. Before leaving for the bedroom, she asked, "What do you do late at night when I'm in there." "I keep watch," he murmured. As if shaking his head over his own incurability he added, "A watch made to the measure of some other's belligerent lookout for lapses." "Who or what is that belligerent other," she cried, thinking of the letter near the television set.

55

Her story ends here. Of course the life, the life with this man, does not end. But that life as a story reducible to story elements ends here. Her story could survive as long as she did not quite accept her life. Now that it is accepted totally without a grain of martyrdom—martyrdom could very well produce difficultites later, the kind that find their way into story elements—there is no longer the need for a story. A story is inconceivable under these conditions of acceptance, of acceptance so deep it cannot be localized. The story could have gone on to include agonizing connections made between her love for this man and her love for her mother, her dim and agonizing discernment of the deplorable similarity between the two figures, her subtle efforts—which under no circumstances are to be vilified as a stratagem, a tactic—to make him renounce the destructiveness of his . . . stratagem—but such inclusions would have caused her to metamorphose into a case history stock figure. At this point—with her retiring and him standing watch over a void—their life rebukes all efforts of the story to capture and partition it into story elements. From now on the life is an apparently homogeneous system where stresses can be in no way sequestered and transmuted into story elements. The life after the story ends is inconceivable as a sum of story elements. It is at once too vastly perceptible and too minutely imperceptible. Whatever changes are worked or not worked cannot be singled out for presentation as elements. They slumber inaccessible. Their life is now a long slumber inaccessible even to themselves. This does not mean however that they are not constantly growing, transforming themselves, enhancing vitality and commitment to each other and to their life together. That life simply resonates at a frequency which is inaccessible to story and its elements.

The Tenement

THE TENEMENT

Sam lived in a tenement. He kept away all day. Up the street the beggars plied.

BEGGARS

Were they inured to the hazards of their vocation, did the clamor in the alleys signify fraternity from which Sam was excluded

SAM

Sam had an excess, of fear and melancholy, to spin off on the centrifuge of days. A task was defining itself slowly. As the task expanded the need for order dwindled. He even began to defend signs of disorder. Or was he trying to assimilate them, widen his idea of order to include them.

MOCK EPIC OF DENUDATION

He had less and less to discard, no longer prey to little panics of acquisition. It was somehow unsatisfactory to throw from a window, denudation fortified only after encountering obstacles, like the reluctance of pawnbrokers.

RETURNING LATE

Would there be a note, not necessarily a letter, merely a note, under the door, pushed so far in not even a ragged edge protruded. A note is rapprochement from and with nowhere.

SPONSORED

He had a small sum to sustain his ministrations to the sick across the bay

MEANS OF TRANSPORT

The scroll of landscape unfurled deep within the bus's glassy flank recapitulated his whole history, the history of his race, a race of one.

ELSA

The proverbial girl next door, dangling the prospect of failure before him in a manner too truly wanton. When he was far from her he had, understandably, to squint to see her and he was also squinting to attenuate what she peddled as radiance.

BEGGAR

At the corner he was accosted. I gave, he said. You don't believe me, he added. You don't believe yourself, said the beggar. It hurt, so much omniscience at midday, the crowds mounting. He looked up, above the willow shag his ferment resumed, it was also underfoot. His smile was phantom signature of attrition. It traversed an infinite distance before casting its shadow over the vicinity of his lips.

THE CITY

Streets incised into its hum, sum of alibis. Was it to him or to what was a little to his right that all referred. He felt the way he assumed a mirror aslant at the bottom of the wall must feel when not only the row of bottles on the sill but also the lights far out into the night are referred to its depth for ratification, parody, effacement.

STREETS

Who let down the streets like tackle from a height.

SAM

Sam was in pursuit but there was no one around inviting capture. He told himself he had come to conquer but mightn't conquest be a pretext for truce, onesided therefore fertile in misgiving.

LOT'S

He looked back to the neon dyspeptic garbling contour

IN THE HALFWAY HOUSE

The patients were waiting for their dose. A fan's shadow was the cubicle's secret pulse.

ELSA

Elsa scrutinized their secretions. She had attained that high point of expertise whence deterioration was discernible less from the content of the piss than from the timbre of the monologue accompanying trickle.

AN OLD MAN

Isn't there always one to complain about the inadequacy of the dosages. He spoke numbly, theatrically. Inflection rendered him fictive, that is to say, beyond the hurt of rehabilitation, yet cried out for help in the fissure between real abjection and limp heroics.

LONG WALKS

Sam's way of proclaiming himself to the addicted was to go a distance from them, make himself missed, feel his absence among them as palpable, swelling. He squinted toward them squinting toward the pinpoint he had yet to become. Then there was the trickle of return, back, to the warm womb of crisis.

FRANZ

Franz became the target of Sam's rehabilitator's fervor. Premonition of inevitably partial failure buoyed him up, was as acute as the premonition of dung in the wake of canines.

ENVY

Sam envied Franz's nod after his dose, declaration of infirmity and embodiment of a selfsufficiency. The nod held desolation at bay, in abeyance.

KEEPERS

To them Sam gave his reports. Sam was dazzled by the addicted. Like a sparrow on a mound he was perched toward the firmament of their collective infirmity, scrutinizing or in terror of homage.

FRANZ

Franz was grateful for his concern, up to a point. He ran the gamut of stances. All he was was merely a foothold toward all he was not and must become to divert his doom. He allowed himself to be, for brief periods only, in order to feel the impingement of all he was not. At a young age, he told Sam, I went mad. The rest is convalescence. He stretched out his arm contemptuously toward everyone else hovering in shadow. How could I not laugh, he continued, seeing them shitting in their pants at the frontier of delirium, recruiting fever and chills toward the blessed volte-face

FRANZ'S VERY OWN KEEPER
This keeper was one of the few whose belly is part and parcel of their cerebral machinery. The keeper's belly metabolized Franz's utterances

FATHERS AND SONS
Franz spoke of his father. From keeper to father involved no leap. My father, Franz began, made counsel pretext for selfpity Don't do as I have done. to thine own self, etc.

TELL ME WHAT I CAN DO TO HELP
Franz often slept in Sam's presence. He awoke to a dew of regret for having divulged so much. Sam was Franz's caretaker and Franz needed a caretaker, someone to be there, to assure him his most virulent acts, that is to say his thoughts, he thought daggers but spoke none. sometimes he had difficulty even thinking them, were not so virulent. He needed someone present to assure him he was never absent, never elsewhere. Sam suited. Yet he was forever goading Sam toward abandonment.

A STAFFMAN SPEAKS
I am a middleman, said Sam. I am tired of backtalk from patients. from superiors. My interrogation is one long cry for help. but I am so at home in my cry for help my cry for help is now a denial of all that prompts cry for help.

PISS
Franz did not like yielding up his piss newly minted for appraisal.

60

FRANZ AND WOMEN

I don't like women. I like their bodies. and it is with rage I tinge my lust when I come upon a birthmark between the breasts. Women rouse you to frenzy then denounce you for excess.

A WALK; A TURNABOUT

Franz questioned Sam about his walk. Sam said of his walk he could not speak because his flaws walked hand in hand with his walks and his flaws he could not enumerate in front of Franz. So Sam let Franz go on proliferating the myth of his keeper's flawlessness in order to butt against it. Franz was silent though his silence stalked, pullulated.

COLLEAGUES GO BY

It is out of Sam's office they are filing where in his absence they have been ransacking his files.

ROOFTOP COMMUNION WITH THE CITY

On the roof Sam waited for Franz to finish his lunch. He waited for the sky's sandbar minutely ribbed to explode into fragments of curd. Did the cloud suck the lifeblood from the city or brood over an anemia. When he enjoyed success with an incorrigible he regenerated the city within himself.

HOMELESS

Franz could no longer tolerate communal life so Sam took him home. The next morning he tried in vain to bring him to the busstop. I have nothing futher to report, Franz said. No incidents, he added. Absence of incident might prove fruitful, said Sam, forcing excavation of the soil truly primal. Franz paced back and forth, never was he out of range. to be out of range would have defeated the purpose of perambulation which was to make an object of his pacing. His reward was the privilege of sneering at his spectator, at his spectator's status of spectator. Franz was shuttling back and forth, back and forth, a cartload of unavowed unavowable woes. He did not want to assault Sam, he wanted every step nullified by absorption into Sam's unflagging omniscience, catalogued before coming fully to birth.

RETURN

The doctors were relieved when Franz finally returned, flanked by Sam.

SAM

Sam had to keep busy in Franz's absence. When Elsa was off duty they coupled. He completed her with his tongue. Was he applying his tongue to the fleece because of the absence of Franz. He tried to subtract Franz absent from the ambience. Franz absent clearly made a difference to the ambience, almost created it. Free of the surveillance exercised by Franz's infirmity he explored his body and that of another, but was the exploration a mere escape from the absence of Franz.

WALK

He passed the railroad track, waiting for the string of cars to pass. He hoped they were loaded even if plenitude condemned them to a preternatural slowness. After they passed he was still waiting, but it was a waiting, he was now aware, of a different order, waiting in the face of bypass, of the stigma of having waited without recompense, without acknowledgment even, for having waited. In short, Sam was abandoned by the cars, empty or full. He tried to appropriate the inflection of his detractors which was, in this case, a rattling roar shot though with shrieks. Detracted he felt closer to his flaws and therefore closer to Franz who was flawed and detained for his flaws.

Now Sam is truly alone, his aloneness no longer a figment molded for the delectation of those opaque to his impersonation of rakish solitaries. Of demon dowagers, of languid ascetics, of young men needy. Sam removed shirt, tie, threw them to the ferns growing between the rails. He felt he was getting to the heart of himself, peeling a few more layers. Beyond the poplars applauded, their motion gapless, less submission to gust than upsurge of intrinsic pulse.

THE LIKES OF FRANZ

The next day he spoke to Franz of his compulsion to be rid of

62

objects. Sometimes, he said, he confused jettison with jettison of the symptom itself, of which these objects were the prop. Franz could not answer, squatting in the middle of the thoroughfare and beating a tattoo on the asphalt. Sam did not understand his role, with Franz on the road to cure once more or beyond cure forever. In any case he did not want Franz interfering with his jettisons. Fealty to the ritual spared him a being taken, by surprise, for in fealty to the ritual of yesterday Sam became yesterday's Sam and therefore knew the denouement of the exploit that was yesterday's Sam.

SLIT IN THE SANDBAG OF BEING
Franz wondered why Sam was afraid of being taken by surprise. Sam explained he did not want to lose sight of time passing losing sight of his gestures for then he would be a mere slit in the sandbag of being oozing through the slit. Franz told Sam he thought it was time for him (Sam) to depart at last.

GETTING FRANZ ACROSS THE BORDERLINE
On the bus out Franz announced he wanted to see his father. Sam recoiled from the father whose pores were large with the glow of health. Franz did tricks for his father. Father grunted before his implausible facsimile. Franz danced attendance on his father's hard stare, sign of omniscience.

THE SPHINX
The father's function was similar to a keeper's: To withhold impressions abounding. Franz was spun about in the centrifuge of the stare. He endured vortex in the hope of better. It was Sam who suggested going. The father waved a fat little hand and said, Good luck. Good luck, schmuck.

THAT NIGHT AND IN THE LAMPLIGHT DOWNED!
Franz slept at Sam's that night. Franz breathed lightly, sometimes his sighs were overpowering as wounds. Next morning it was Franz who woke Sam and who missed the halfway house. Franz dressed. Every time he lifted another article he almost fell over gaping. as if to regurgitate a night's chimeras.

RETURN TO THE HH

When the couple arrived it was midmorning. The keeper said, Tell me about your day. The keeper smiled, his remark resonating with self-congratulation, professionally subdued. For he had succeeded in making a remark that obtunded both their bulks and errancies, forced them to meet exclusively in the world of words. Sam, you may go, said the keeper, though by no means of higher echelon. Saying, you may go, unchallenged, he created his precedence on the spot. It was to this sentence he owed his promotion.

As Sam closed the door he strained for a sight of himself in the glass, not because he was vain, he merely needed to be reconstituted for the, you may go, made splinters where Sam had been. Before going to his immediate superior with his weekly report he went to the john. Above the sink was a mirror. He followed the lesion going from upper lip to nostril. He must wait until the lesion disappeared before appearing before the superior. Sam did not waltz into the future the way an islet of foam waltzes itself to the rim of a coffee cup. He incubated the future, standing still. Its beginning would be lesions' unattainable end at last attained.

A FIELD

Behind the halfway house Franz asked, dazzled by the sun or Sam's truancy, Can you just leave them. Sam shrugged. What did you tell the keeper, Sam asked. Why must I have told him, Franz asked. Do you think I unfold a case history for every comer. Sam discerned Franz fought off his words almost as ardently as he fought to bring them to birth.

A STRANGE TIME OF DAY

A strange time of day, Sam said, as they walked. There were things Sam could say walking he could not say standing still for when walking he was walking away from what he said and from the one to whom he said. Franz collapsed. Sam advanced but suddenly Franz was raging against Sam's collusion with all those who decreased the dosage stepwise. He rose then collapsed, then collapsed again, forever on the verge of departure, perhaps if he could only finally master departure there would be no need for voyage. Get up, Sam said. I don't want to be your caretaker. Franz got up saying he would go to his father. Your father, Sam spewed. The son finds an alibi for stasis in the desolation of the father, the father puts to sleep, with gestures rotary, abysmal, the will of the son. Franz ran then walked, as if abutting on dreamless sleep.

PARTING GIFTS
Franz departed and Sam incubated a grief, the grief that descends whenever the need to act becomes too clear. Sam wanted to throw off a carapace compacted of centuries of hesitation, laced with a little self-loathing. He slept. When he awoke he leaped out of bed and down the stairs into the street where the branches were livid against the streetlamp glow.
He went out. He went to the bus stop at which Elsa was alighting. He led her back but all the way back he told himself he was not, he was merely returning to his room, his bed, his pillow, its fosse. Sam spoke of-the only matter that concerned him, Franz.

SPEAKING OF FRANZ
And how is he getting on, Elsa asked, keeping step. He wanted to answer but not too discreetly. He wanted to revolt her and then she would diagnose him thereby deflected from her to diagnosis. Then when he was a little at home with the diagnosis he could throw it back as if a patent absurdity all the time panting for retraction. She engaged in sexual relations with him to allay his fears about Franz. He was in debt afterwards in some undefinable way but his fears were not allayed. She overpowered him, more than ever he felt drawn to Franz as he disengaged himself, perhaps he was not drawn to Franz, perhaps he was only disengaging himself from Elsa. He could not tell where she ended and he began. Such disorientation exhilarates for brief intervals. Sam was at once accessible and inaccessible to Sam in Franz. The Sam recoiling from Elsa was buried in the depths of Franz, who must be retrieved.

65

ELSA LEAVES

She left him. He could not sleep on sheets bearing her body's imprint, ravaged by the glue of her odors. He went next day to the bay's edge, bathed himself clean.

THE BAY

This domain pacified because though the strands stretched one way and the sea pulsed the other way there was a boundary, between sand and sea, or rather the incessant dissolution of a boundary, hammock of the slack and the limp. There Sam met Franz. Franz's ribs rose as the wavelets rose and fell. The sun gloated over the shoals.

SAM INTERROGATES FRANZ WHO IS HAPPY HERE

Franz had sectored off the shore into a new country, jealous of its climate and mores. The wind was mild, almost implicit. They set out. Sam became afflicted with a symptom. The symptom reduced all sounds to the common denominator of honed importunity. Sam was not yet acquainted with the symptom but he conjectured relief would involve pitchers.

ON THE BUS HEADING SOUTH

Sam made gestures on the bus. Why did one gesture relieve, another exacerbate. He asked the other passengers, was there a rest room. From their queasiness he pieced together a general direction. In the rest room the flux of things slowed and he nested in the folds of the flux. He was cured until the next time, the next john. For the time being he was cured, that is to say for a little eternity for life is a succession of infinitesimal intervals into each of which he burrowed for all he was worth. Relieved he nevertheless felt about to be waked into the stench of an irrevocable incontinence. By shifting his position an oblong of reflected light was transmuted into an ooze, ductile, exiguous.

BUS STOPS IN A FOREIGN LAND

Sam left Franz among the fruit stalls and began looking for work. Pacing did not exercise proprietary right over orchards of trash. Absence of others on sidestreets pierced like a dagger. Here he

66

was suffering the instant resurrection of every pore sensitized. Every pore became an eye therefore he was a multiplicity of gashes gaping. He was veering toward coincidence with himself, felt the tightening of the straitjacket that was his own skin, the tightening consigned him to an unsuspected freedom, to live in the moment. No longer a future of mammoth reparation contingent on an unflinching abstention.

WAIT TILL I GET BACK AND TELL FRANZ ABOUT THIS. BOY WILL HE BE.

Sam chose to work in a pit. Every night before turning in Sam said, Get a job. But Franz was afraid of jobs because afraid of mastery, he was best as apprentice, effacing himself and his handiwork with a silence boding some future bound untrammelled. Learn to draw blood, Sam said, punching his pillow and consigning his skull to the recess.

RIPPLE

The seasons came and went with disquieting regularity. And Franz let them, forever abdicating. Franz thought sometimes the solution was to rid himself of objects. But Sam was now attached to their few acquisitions. It was futile anyway, Franz knew, from his little experience of denudation, for when you believe you have achieved an ideal minimum you are suddenly confronted with the plenitude in the depths of the pane. And then there is the moon, elusive target of inventory, horned and astrut the tightrope of boughs. Little of Sam's skill transfused to Franz.

FRANZ RECUMBENT

Franz took to lying in the pit as Sam worked to support them. Franz went on inviting diagnosis the way others invite a sock in the jaw. Working cured Sam of a need to be diagnosed, at least incessantly. Franz tried to run off with the money earned.

SAM'S SEARCH

Sam was obliged to go out looking for Franz, found him in a clearing. Sam demanded an explanation. Franz took refuge in a flawless chronology of all that had happened, was still happening to him. I'm looking for a vocation that does not thrive on failure in other spheres, he said. Franz was undernourished and liking it, his balls wizened plums. I am fettered to a penance, he said. which bears with the dawning of each day less and less of a relation to the trespass on whose behalf it was spawned. Where is the ultimate diagnosis, he concluded. I will not provide it. Sam said, because your future will attempt to elude and in eluding discredit it. Diagnosis, diagnosis, Franz whispered. sinking fast. Are you afraid of administering the last opiate lest I become addicted in my terminal state, Franz said. He laughed so loud Sam was afraid they would both be swallowed up. I arrived too late. Sam said, searching for twigs from which to stitch a headrest. What good were you as a keeper, Franz said. Say, What good are you as a keeper, Sam pleaded. Why do keepers congregate where symptoms are minimal. Here, in this clearing, where there is a veritable proliferation, that is to say here I am, there are none. Try to go on. Sam said, raising Franz's head to accommodate the stitchwork. Why bother, Franz said. I have played out all possible denouements. And if I were to, go on that is, would you know how to cure me of convalescence, could you minister to the symptoms dawning when it dawns on me I am long for this world. You want me to go on for who is so ideally suited for a certain corner of the halfway house. If I rehabilitated myself here you and your ilk would be offended. Tell them that just before I sank never to rebound I heard the reparative tissue folding over the lesion. Sam looked up at the sky. You look at the sky because I look at you, Franz said. Sam said his looking did not cause his looking, but was merely a precondition for such looking. I rage at you. Franz said, then I rage at you for making me rage, in flagrant contravention of this distance. dearly won. from rage, from rapture too, from all stances insisting that I situate myself here anew. that I be.

A Day in the Life of an Uninvited Guest

I have been a servant here for too long. There are times when I feel like a guest. So that I am both servant and guest. I do not make a habit of unnecessary ambiguity. But I am certain there are times when I am waiting to be served and that waiting plausible to and encouraged by the others. The rest of the time I am serving, huffing and puffing above the hot plate. The walls are beginning to crumble and the masters will soon be departing. Sometimes I feel these are not the real masters but that the masters will appear someday and when they appear their demands will be different, their tone will be at once more deferential and more difficult.

This morning I was returning from the outhouse in the middle of the wheat and saw a pigeon reflected in a puddle. Then the pigeon moved away. I wondered as I walked why the pigeon moved away, was it from the puddle or was it from the reflection. Was it trying to deprive me of its reflection, I who have so little. I who have so little. Delete. Just because I am a servant does not mean I must speak like a servant.

One of the masters' children was running in the distance. Not the one getting married to a member of another tribe. Perhaps this one was running from the imminent catastrophe. But lovers need an overlay of heterogeneity, I always say. And it is easy for me to say because I have never been a lover and do not intend to be, especially now, with my sagging skin. I belong among the androgynes, clawing the walls of their cells. Unions are always difficult among our people, in any case, and here at least dissension among the two families will be provoked by a relatively clear-cut obstacle.

69

I decided to return late that morning, to avoid my masters assembled on the staircase. In these parts the sunrise is celebrated. They celebrate the clarity of dawn, treetops violaceous against the bruise. They mistake clarity of outline for the far more difficult clarity of each individual leaf of each individual branch. But they tell themselves by telling each other that the venation can be discerned. Simply because the frontier between tree and sky jumps to the eye. Frontier between tree and sky is the serrated edge of night. And remark their phrasing: The venation can be discerned. Impeccably vague. The children do not stand still easily. They threaten to dismember the balustrade. Parents pretend not to hear so given up to rapture are they. For rapture they must feign. Rapturous they cannot be overtaken by the deities they fear, deities inhabiting the venation of each leaf of each branch of each bough of each trunk of each tree of each wood resounding with the woodcutters' vehemence.

I was returning from the outhouse musing when I saw the child running against the horizon. I passed shops on the way back. I noticed in one a picture of a clairvoyante. Not La Sosostris. In her hands was posed the hand of one succumbing uncritically to her omniscience. Clear from the angle between thumb and forefinger he was amorous of her omniscience. Her omniscience was palpable. It ascended like fumes. She fondled that hand and at the same time she assessed the weight in grams of his credulity. One hand buoyed up the wrist and the other fingered all that was not wrist.

If I had not seen the child and deduced the presence of its parents (nearby) from its frantic motions I might never have stopped for the photograph, to invest it with all it did not possess. Passing the shop I had the look of one who conceals what he has seen or better who has survived beyond his seeing into the icy privilege with which secret seeing invests him.

I pretended to be a little dazed from the sun or rather from the midday haze. It was midday. I decree a midday steeped in haze the way tea is steeped in shrub detritus. I passed tourists. Since they behaved like tourists I had to behave like a denizen. I looked around like one jaded by all he refuses to see still one more time. They weren't fooled.

They named our landmarks in their own tongue. I did not know how I felt about having the outhouses appropriated. Or rather I did not know how the masters expected me to feel when cherished syllables were mauled. Their syllables seemed a purposeful deformation of our own.

I got on the bus, the local, Number 2535EJ-rh4Xqt. I wanted to mingle with other denizens. But once I had no desire to mingle or rather once mingling I could not connect the activity with "mingling" because the activity was nothing like what I had imagined saying "mingling". Though strictly speaking I was not imagining when I said "mingling". Rather I was stepping on the toes of imagining. Mingling left no room for "mingling". Instead I chose to be dazzled by the familiar: Billboard, tree, haze. The bus denizens were perplexed. I waved their obtuseness away. Or rather the bus waved it away with each jolt, wiped clean the slate of my unintelligibility. I was grateful for the hummocks that made for jolts.

The child was a pinpoint on the horizon. Riot within.

My own fate at the hands of the masters reflected in the pool of diminution? It was still running but now it was running not away not towards but against, I was glad for the riot, not that it was anything like Myshkin's rapture before the froth, I don't want you to think that, I don't want you to envy me, don't think I want you to envy me, don't envy me. Concentrate on the void not on the dazzling replenishment of that void. I throw phrases to the leonine void.

The void makes martyrs of my phrases. Shades of antiquity, there. Yes, I forgot to mention that the surname of my masters was Shades. And their country of origin and dissolution, Antiquity. Address all enquiries to the Shades of Antiquity.

Back on the bus I tried to be more amiable. How far from the Shades, I asked. I sounded like a tourist. I cannot say I tried to sound like a tourist. But among denizens I seem like a tourist and among tourists like a denizen. The denizen started answering me. I was terrified. For didn't he understand that I asked a question not because I expected an answer. Even though I looked hard at him pretending to be drinking it all in, the way a poplar half shorn drinks deep of autumn shadow. Finally it ended. I turned to the window. There were poplars in the window. There was occasion for rapture. How do I know it was rapture. I had to piss with nothing to piss. That is rapture. Such is rapture. I described what I saw to those around me. One of them asked a relevant, that is to say, an agonizing question. Why tell, he said. To preserve, I said. Or supplant, he said. His thrusts were coy though he was not coy. I tried to invest him with the coyness his thrusts embodied. I couldn't answer. Riot once more.

I thought of my masters. When I am overwhelmed I think of my masters and consider them responsible for the fact that I am easily overwhelmed. I inveigh against thinking that I am warding them off, flaunting my liberty.

The masters were responsible for my having to fuck more than once. Fucking for the first time I pared away all the fat of the inessential or essential, I never knew which. Fucking for the second time, immediately after, I played variations on the theme of fucking's essence. Fucking for the first time I was too busy proving myself once again capable. The first fuck was a tidal wave and in the end represented by the second fuck's commencement I began to think about myself performing the act and how I could swerve from the protocol of the first fuck. I deformed it mercilessly, refused to follow in its footsteps, commented ironically. In the second fuck I mauled fucking. I mauled my self of the first fuck. But I could never be sure whether in repeating the act I was approaching closer and closer to its essence or whether having achieved essence in the first fuck I was now merely nibbling at its fritters. On such problems hells are founded.

Yet there were times in the course of my journey by bus, for we are still bus-ridden, we are bus-ridden until I permit the driver to permit me to descend into the muddy fartpath, when I forgot the masters, thought of them as passed or rather of the hurt they had inflicted as passed. I was no longer indissolubly bound to the hurt. And what of the good they did, you might ask.

Not only might you ask for you do ask, you are asking, I can hear you, even this far away. And do you ask because you want me to see both sides of the matter or rather are you merely eager to provoke me. The good.

Once they said of the shit on the fartpaths, The shit is not so good here but it smells okay in summertime. In that sentence they disposed of the shit once and for all. I had believed for so long that before you can dispose of shit in that manner or any other you must undergo a laborious apprenticeship to shit-tasting, shit-kicking, shit-smelling. I was forever approaching a little nearer to the shits. I was Zeno and shit the tortoise. And here they were, those masters, disposing not only of the shit but of apprenticeship to the shit and everything that is not shit, in a single sentence. They showed me without intending to show me, they showed me bypassing me, as it were, that one needn't be forever on the road toward, to count for something.

At first I took them for depleted because they were not striving, as I was striving, toward a better, or rather a keener, appreciation of shit. But they had a sentence that they wielded like a sceptre. And the sceptre cleared them, the Shades, a path toward wholeness. They weren't seeking plenitude in crippled worship of the fartpath shits. They wielded their leanness of a single sentence uttered without fanfare like a plenitude. They wielded a plenitude. The sentence was as imperishable as—an erect cock. And never would I look at the shits in the same way again. So there you have the good living after them. Though they are not dead yet. And once

And once I saw a horse alone in the meadow. I discerned a goat sniffing its balls. And one of the masters said quite casually, from his barouche, pointing out the spectacle of the horse and the goat in the meadow to a neighbor, a distant cousin, come to visit, A goat accompanies it sometimes. And in that sentence horse and goat were recuperated. I looked back at goat and horse. The goat tripped crippled after the horse's clanging balls. But the sentence that resurrected them or killed them or killed then resurrected them rose up proud as a stallion. I forgave the master his barouche. I was a communist at the time.

The bus was swerving to a halt. No more need to piss. I raised my forefinger to my eyebrow, as some Czech once prescribed, and that gesture liberated the question, no doubt eternal, What gesture capsizes the feeble equilibrium postponing release of piss into the world's damp forepocket. I neared the broken fence that marks the onset of the masters' terrain. I was terrified at the prospect of meeting the masters even though it was for the 6753848374848584th time. Because I could not get a foothold in my terror I decided I was incapable of feeling. Therefore I was now terrified at my lack of feeling. And the only relief from the terror at lack of feeling was the prospect of the family's antics. Prospect, since the antics themselves were always stale.

But terror at lack of feeling became more terrifying than terror at meeting the family. At least terror of the family was terror of. Terra firma. Once I recognized or accepted or decreed my terror to be terror of the family I could experiment. I had a foothold at last. With one foot in the door of terror I could proliferate other versions of terror. I was terrified of shit, farts, tenderness.

Before returning I decided to cut my hair. Pustules littered my visage. Sometimes its hard to say face. Did the cutting cause a physiological imbalance which manifested itself as ripe-strawberry syndrome, or did rearrangement of less than hyacin-thine locks accentuate merely latent blemishes. I went out into the sun. Bronze cancels blemish. But I could not permit myself to stay away long from the shade of the great halls. Not that I had an unnatural hunger for marble and sconces. But the shade of the great halls is conducive to masturbation and I had, at that moment (the sun high in the sky), a craving to be one with myself. I felt that by dreaming of sconces I blemished my imminent walk into the sun.

Then I said, He liked to go into the sun. With that sentence I reconstituted going, I made going possible. I sought then not the sun but what the sentence outlined of going, drooping, bathing. I walked and walked waiting with bated breath for the slice of activity corresponding to, He liked to go into the sun. Then I mutilated my going because it did not correspond, in no way did it correspond, to the going promised by the sentence which I dare not repeat lest nostalgia resurge uncontrollably in every wasted faculty and fibre.

I told the cows in the courtyard I was ambivalent about going. They turned away. They blinked their tormentors away from their long-lidded eyes.

They jingled their bells. They mooed. They did everything they could do to convince me summer was still in favor with the firmament. But they would have nothing of my protestations of ambivalence. I envied their contentment, stunned, piebald. The masters had their own cows then. Delete the "then" as if they don't have cows now or as if they don't have their own cows now. Apparently I am trying to induce your tear for the cows dead or confiscated. As if their not having cows now reflects some inexplicable convulsion in the world. I smuggle my own nostalgia (for what?) into a sentence that celebrates (in an undertone) the unsung nostalgia of others. I lame them. I was about to add, for what they did to me, but I would probably try to lame them anyway. The bus came to a halt. I descended. In descending I wept. Having been separated from the masters a whole morning long I missed them. It is absence and absence only that importunes affirming thereby the stratum in which we are bound, inseparably, the masters and I, you and I, you and the masters, the good masters and the bad, and which we are bound intermittently to forget.

I put parcels on the kitchen table, to remind them of my usefulness. In the outhouse, a national landmark, I pull down my pants and align my cheeks with the cold, dewy seat. Now I can better appreciate the parcels left unwrapped on the kitchen table. They speak for me. They sing. I anticipate the collision of the

75

masters with those parcels. I am indebted to their eloquence. Shitting loudly I muffle the strains of that eloquence. Outbursts in the outhouse merit a chapter to themselves, several chapters, a chapter that inundates all other chapters, the pauses passing for chapters.

In the outhouse I am still squatting, awaiting the masters. The masters are not ashamed of their pustules as I am. They do not even experience that tortured bravado that is shame. They talk not only with mouths but with pustules, recruiting all their deformities into the heyday, the fray. I love my masters as I love their deformities as I love the niches in the stucco facade, refuge for minor deities, deities unconnected in our minds with fire and brimstone. I love the country house though I'll soon be leaving, oh yes 3546374757475 years is quite enough thank you. Because I'll soon be leaving. It is a pleasure to know that whatever you are doing at a particular moment is festooned with simultaneities. While you are masturbating you can be sure another is shitting. A third is knitting. A fourth is licking crumbs off his chipped saucer in the refectory. Adrift in a warm current of simultaneities. And what lovelier sound than that of the family eating, belching, farting, parting its collective lips in ridicule of the scapegoat for the day, as I am preparing the next course in the windowless kitchen. They were afraid a window might distract me from.

Eyes are enough, one was heard to say, closing his in rapt anticipation of my sunless misery. Was it Fucky, who said that, or Willie, devoted paramour of Lucky, sobsister to Jerrie, six feet under Louie, who tormented Pukey with the imminence not of his death but of his decline. His decline, imagine, and he was only ninety. It is hard to say since though Fucky was married to Pukey she was also granddaughter of Yekkie. So that when Fucky called Lucky brother instead of mother it was not merely a not uncommon familial lapse on the verbal level. For Fucky was, in fact, both the sister and the son of Lucky. Lapses everywhere, in the outhouse too.

76

I for one heard best in the outhouse. I heard not actual conversations but the shadows of conversations. I heard one say to another, perhaps it was Pukey to Lukey, not Lucky, Lukey, that he had a completely twisted vision of the world. Yet it was precisely Pukey whose vision was twisted and what is more he knew he himself was guilty of the attribution he squandered so carelessly but he needed to be able to speak of himself and yet seem not to be speaking of himself. He had no alternative but to invent the frailty of Lukey, godfather of Tuk-Ee.

There was another who told stories and irrigated their bald spots with digressions. But he always cut off digressions at their root or their peak with a sigh, and the expression, What does it matter. And the, What does it matter, impugned less his ungovernable garrulity than the failure of the listener to support the text, or the failure of discourse itself to bear up boldly under the strain of secondary and tertiary tensions. And he sank these subspecies of the essential. There was a third or a fourth who, having listened to a statement of the form I cannot do X, from Duky, would reply, What's wrong with doing X. Was he genuinely perplexed or was he merely prompting, basely, the details of an incompetence.

But sometimes the sound of my shitting (I cannot say the sound of my shit since sometimes I rumbled without extruding) cancelled the shadow of the sound of conversation or the sound of the shadow. Sometimes my shame at shitting profusely or needing to shit and being unable prevented me from listening. And when I came back from the outhouse to take my place at the table I could never tell whether all or any of those assembled had heard me at it. Some faces expressed recoil but was it recoil from what they had heard me doing or from my long absence which seeded discord. In short, I was an umpire.

One of them suggested I was in mourning. The patriarch, an experienced mourner, having outlived most of his family, most of his race, asked, but no one in particular, how I could be in mourning since I was not ALL IN BLACK. His eldest son explained there were other ways to mourn. Some mourn through excessive preoccupation with whether or not they have locked the outhouse door after the load is laid.

The eldest son explained that I took so long returning because I was so preoccupied. I locked the outhouse because though a servant I knew it contained valuables. In addition, I did not want the odor of my shit to penetrate the dining hall. I hurried for tasks awaited me but I became so absorbed in locking that locking became the endpoint of all exploit. I forgot the baking and dusting. And then when the time available was considerably reduced I returned to my tasks and found that though I had to rush I stretched each out to the crack of doom, like putty, so engrossed did I become. I could not extricate myself from the deceleration. It seemed I was performing them badly and so I had to repeat certain steps and yet each repetition became an impediment on the way to competent repetition. Such was mourning. Eldest sons rarely err. And what is he mourning, asked the father of his goblet, half full. He seemed to be contemplating the question melancholically. Perhaps to disguise his bald curiosity. For the father was more than a father, he was patriarch, a magnate, and he was supposed to be immune from curiosity. He wanted his sons to grow up tall and strong and hairy chested. Yet he had them dressed preciously, up to a certain period he wanted to emphasize the softness of their infant contours. And now they were literally jumping out of their skins for they were stigmatized for the scars of that preciosity before their comrades. So they developed a power in debate as they awaited the hair on chest, balls and asses, as they awaited for fat to fall from thighs and forearms. I saw them waiting at the beach. When no one was looking they did not swim or kick sand in each other's eyes, they sat and waited for manhood, gathered shells for the kitchen table, shells as libation for the god of latent manhood, no minor deity, or minor after all. The patriarch's question was never answered.

We followed him out into the garden. The competition of branches diverging from a single bole for a single ray of sun accounted for the contrapposto. The sons knew my ambivalence _apropos of servants and masters. They mimicked my ambivalence. They seemed at sea apropos of vocations. But I heard their professions with the contemptuous skepticism of an inventor who stumbles everywhere on bad copies pregnant with homage. I had invented ambivalence, or rather I and I alone had raised it to the status of a sentiment. And here they were

I was in the garden, a world of objects resembling those of the world without. Sometimes it seemed to me inconceivable that in a world where a pine cone dozed there could subsist also a foxglove, a cat's cry, a shit. I tried not to believe that the presence of object A cancelled the possibility of object B, if not exactly adjacent then at least nearby. I tried to explain my fear of the garden's inability to accommodate so many disparate objects to the most precocious of the eighteen sons. He held back. And when it seemed for all his holding back he understood I cried out, Do you understand. But there was something false in my crying out for I knew very well at that point he understood, otherwise I would never have asked, or rather cried out with such triumphant disbelief. For I cry out, Do you understand, only to conceal the horror at being so well understood, understood beyond appeal, if you like. Understood I am robbed the way a Vermeerian cubicle is robbed of nacre by a too avid laugh. And I am always afraid of being understood better than I understand myself, so I cry out, Do you understand, better to topple the other's leaning tower of lucidity. He smiled a little. The cypresses shook. Did they too understand or were they merely amused at my mulish attempts to rob others.

The precocious son, son number B, moved a little distance away. I planned what I would say to him when he came back. But when he came back I no longer had any desire to say what I had rehearsed because it was rehearsed. I would be inflicting artifice on an inno-cent and yet I had planned what I would say to him during his absence precisely to prove that I had not been ill-intentioned, secretive. No escape from artifice. I decided to scuttle all I had intended to yield up and improvise. I thought of speaking of my concept of an ideal fucking, the first and the second, but it seemed to me I would be disguising the real obsession by speaking of fucking. "Fucking" was a placeholder. I placed it in the sentence because I needed to make the sentence in order to be swept along by it, in order to trace a certain curve inside myself speaking the sentence. Thus, fucking. Yet perhaps I was most myself speaking of fucking. Speaking of fucking, perhaps I was most myself. Here I was, a mere country boy, thinking I was escaping myself speaking of fucking, pouncing on the most colorless of words, of TERMS, and all along I was being reunited with myself, that is to say with my primary obsession. But perhaps when I spoke of fucking in this manner I was not speaking of fucking in the realm where we love, loathe, know it. By dint of repetition I was further from fucking than I had ever been. An if anyone AT THAT POINT dares suggest that the subject of my discourse was essentially cock, balls, and cunt wet with hunger, I will recoil, stunned, authentically dumbfounded. Get back in the narrative, get back. But none of the sons wanted to hear about fucking even if fucking was not the true subject of discourse. Fucking was signpost and impediment on the way to the true subject. The sons, in any case, wanted to fuck. They scratched their balls, unknowing. I tore at my balls with my nails. I tore at my balls because I wanted to tear at the balls of another, who may or may not have owned balls as we know them. I hurt myself. But do not believe I hurt myself. Or at least do not believe I hurt myself now because in writing "I hurt myself" I compensate myself for all the hurt of long ago and yesterday. Long ago I signed a covenant in blood (and in the juices of my puberty), a covenant between my pain and my language. The covenant has survived periods of unrest. For every paid inflicted (inflicter irrelevant) I was guaranteed a sentence, a turn of phrase, whose onset and subsiding narcotized me until (for?) the next onslaught. I envied the sons being able to scratch their balls without knowing they scratched, without allowing themselves to know others were watching. For they could set aside certain acts as burrows into which they retreated digging, kicking away from the world. and from whose capsized coign they spied. Tearing at my balls he—I was always conscious of the imminence of others. At any moment a glance might penetrate to the depth of my ostensible self-absorption so that I was both in and out of the tearing at my balls. But I was never totally inside the tearing as the others were, as the brothers were. But I am no brother, no. I wanted to talk about fucking but can I blame them for recoiling when they hardly knew if I was talking as servant or guest. As guest my expatiation would have been acceptable but as servant I could only have been wishing to extract their vital juices. How could I convince them of my good intentions. I spoke to them of my origins, the little house on the big mainland, front slightly corrugated, hint of undulation amid all that rigidity. I felt I was winning them over to wonderment at a distant phenomenon. Canopies like probosces, I added.

Describing the mainland was a way of getting off the island. Reverie did not last. The matriarch called me back. She warmed to me only when I renounced my right to guestdom. The sons were powerless against her. I trudged toward the kitchen where a heap of unpeeled tomatoes awaited me. She telephoned from the next room to ask what I was doing. Nothing, she answered. Long and hard pause before the Nothing. A fruit, its plummet overshot the overripeness of my expectation. In fact, I had been masturbating. I was not sure whether masturbation qualified as nothing. Did she know I had, in fact, been masturbating. And if she knew did her verdict forcibly encompass masturbation. And if she did not know did her verdict encompass it anyway. For sometimes masturbation struck me (struck me!) as a plenitude.

She came in to inspect my fingers. Dread of dirty nails, she added. She nodded toward the bloody foodstuffs. Foodstuffs, she summarized, looking me straight in the eye, straight up the ass, what difference does it make. What disconcerted was her gaze surviv-

81

ing her utterance. Did she have something more to say or was she waiting for me to say something. I continued peeling and I refused to subordinate peeling to waiting. Finally, she said, You would never marry outside the tribe. Did she admire or despise me. I did not reply, I slowed up my peeling as if pondering. She apologized for the kitchen. Then she apologized for the house itself. Finally the island. We are not Australia, she said. She strove for a mutual connivance in the face of an insufficiency that did and did not concern us. Even islands have their hierarchy, and the smallest partakes of and is smothered by the splendor of the largest. What she implied was that our island would someday be Australia or rather in its uniqueness the island was quite content not to be Australia but believed that a token deference, intermittently, enhanced its superiority. To reassure her I said, I like your island. Immediately I was assaulted by all aspects of the island I did not like. For to say, I like your island, was to be infinitely close to the matriarch. I had to catalyze a cleavage. And yet a comment like, I like your island, converted me to a simple man, because my sentence was simple. Moreover, it procured me an unguided tour of the island and a haphazard inventory of its slender riches. In my zeal to prove myself wrong, false, contemptible, or simply inaccurate, far from her love, I summoned up remembrance of its coves, swamps, shitheaps, sunsets. I couldn't decide whether my comment was true or false. Perhaps I had meant to say, I like your island am lost at sea.

Neighbors approached. I saw them through the kitchen window. She pretended not to have seen them or rather have heard since she was far from the tiny porthole that passed for a window in what passed for my domain. She pretended her exit was casual, somnabulist even. I too wanted to exit. I was tired of faces for I had reached that point in life where every new face seems like a labored ingenuity, a facile juxtaposition of features already known, run through, discarded. A last leap at novelty. Clearly she did not see them that way because I could hear her in the sickroom, making ready to hold court. Before they entered she brought me a pair of gloves. For now she was courted she needed to atone for her good fortune. Alone she neglected me mercilessly, unable to foresee her heady contrition. So there she was with her gloves, smile warring with grimace. The island is changing, she told me, helping me on with them. Foreigners, all foreigners, Arabs, Jews, blacks, mulattoes, Creoles. In short, implausible coupling and its aftercourse. Perhaps she felt obliged to inveigh AGAINST to conceal her love of humanity incarnated in her guests. She left me to the tomatoes. I didn't ask if the tomatoes were for the guests. Was I peeling for the guests or for some far-off family affair. Left in the lurch, as always.

I held up the skins before my eyes but no nymphs on the other side. Using gloves I had to strain to distinguish textures. Without gloves I assimilated textures all in a heap, I could not tell them from my own skin's. Clearly the gloves were useful. They marked a stage in my apprenticeship. To what. At the same time I felt the gloves crowding me out. They had no use for my fingers. Did they discard my fingers or swallow them up. The gloves improved my peeling and wiped it out. As I peeled I felt I was getting back to her, winning her away from her guests. And at the same time I felt I was trying to lose her among my work. In my vocation, I added, laughing, dropping the skins in a fit of hilarity. And peeling was I coping with her absence or evading my anguish over her absence. Immersed once more in a warm bath of doubt. With a little encouragement I could have wept salts into the tub.

To my delight to the original pile of unpeeled tomatoes was opposed a heap of unskinned. I could hardly distinguish her voice among those of her guests, everybody making hay at once. For that is what it is to be alive, try to distinguish yourself from the others. They stamped their feet, clapped their hands. For how do you know what are YOUR arms and legs with so many going at once.

Origin

What was it possessed my going, to appear, make myself known. It wasn't a long journey though when it began to appear so I stopped to tame what threatened to proceed without me. Then I moved on. When the door opened the head of household turned toward me as the rest of him maintained allegiance to the direction of interrupted movement. His lady gave me her full attention in stupefaction. I could tell she was thinking fast. I enjoyed the discomfiture, I prey on loose ends. The children referred to the parents who had nothing, absolutely nothing, to offer in the way of imitable posture. I had to come, I said. Or rather I've come to discover what propulsively populates my labors without my knowing—what allows them to go by the name of labors. And I think I know I owe the very existence of these populators to you. I laughed heartily, no one asked why, I told them. I've come presumably to unearth my origin when all along, it is true, I've been loving what sidesteps its stench. Or it is not so much my origin I come seeking as the axioms that have regulated my postponement of the quest. I saw I was making them tic-ridden. Semi-collapsed, the mother said, Why did you come. You were, if you must know, the fruit not of a union but of a sundering. I had almost succeeded in yanking myself free when the seed spilled. He took my curses for coquettry. And you're just like him. I'll stand my ground as long as I have to, I said. For what purpose, said a daughter. I wanted to see you, I said still to the lady of the house. The husband turned away, clearly he could not bear the sight of me as well as whatever else of my marginal being was visited upon his sensorium. Suddenly he turned to her and implored, I thought all this was over and done with. It was, came the dead cadence. And now it's starting all over again. I could have hugged her not because she was any more reconciled but rather because she was the first, the very first, to perceive, that is proclaim, and thereby induce, a modification in present circumstances. Could you have tolerated it if I hadn't come, never came, I asked. We've tolerated it pretty well this far. The fact of her answering—never mind the spurning content—demonstrated how rapidly she had assimilated my . . . inconceivableness. So what if her inflection did not care in the least to know she was very possibly just a wee bit glad to smell her breath in my own. Go away. How can I, I countered. I want you to wait with me as the signposts trudge past my explorations. It's good you have so rich a love of adventure, was the sneering observation. How I loathe life, I recited. Before completing my utterance I was already assaulted with too many instances proving conclusively I was not so loath to be as, here on their threshhold, I professed. How I loathe life, how I loathe the laws of life. Adding that last I marred sufficiently the all too predictable contour she might knead from the stuff of this declamation. I became . . . unlocalizable. But you folks, I intruded. What about us, growled the husband, shooting straight from the hip. You're what I always dreamed you'd be. Yes, I added. I made as if to draw into my ken, if not my arms, all those presently in, or on the verge of, flight. Stop, no stop, said one, the daughter who had spoken before. The others drew back. Are we really what you always hoped for, she insisted. All so beautiful, I lisped, so fully formed. Look at you, a magnificent tableau vivant, a pocket of eternity not two steps from the city dump. I simply can't get over it—you—all of you—not just you and you and you. Husband and father thawed a little, tried to draw closer to the heart of the brood, stroked here a hip, there a wrist. Remembering me, however, he said without focusing, Why

86

don't you just get lost. His trouble is, said wife, said mother—mine—he can't. He's fixed, localized beyond appeal. Bound—all too utterably bound—to prostration before what he takes—must take—to be glaringly antidotally alternative to—the laws of life. What will happen when he discovers that I—we—his tormentors—are by no means to be considered capable of assisting the flight from a plaguey accountability to those laws. I felt myself warming, I longed to contribute to the diagnosis, to fuse with her in its folds, the longing died. Rather than confront you, true target of rage, I prefer to campaign for your recruitment in coalition against some other—out there. Night and its aftermath came and went many times before any of them found the courage to crawl toward the verge of asking, What—out there.

Hut Man

I decided to come down from the hills where I worked. It did not amount to much but I cherished it. And I liked the view of the river and its hills beyond. In the hills there are animals, little flowers, shanties, and a long dusk. There is a first dusk and then another, recapitulation of all that has come before. When work was done and I was too tired to be attentive to the first dusk and its lessons I waited for the second dusk, which came unsolicited by vigilance. This dusk made it a point to smother the last of the little flowers, no more than remnants of the cows' long dinner. Cows, then goats. The goats were wary of the cows. Though the cows seemed serenely vexed by flies through their haze and beneath the gaze stifled by the haze there was a rage, surprisingly petty, and infinitely more virulent than the gazing forbearing smouldering. The goats knew that the petty lacerating rage would ultimately win out over the forbearing, punctuated rarely by blinks. Waiting until the cows were gone the goats ate the blooming roots anointed with their spittle. And the taste was good, the goats agreed, because they persisted in the chewing without looking up or to the side or toward the sky darkeningly ravaged by a pelt, now blue, now black. The cows came in the first dusk and the goats in the second, though it is incorrect to say the goats emerging from the thicket marked the second dusk's beginning. Nor is it correct to say the passing of the cows marked the end of the first dusk. Yet it is no more correct to assume that the transition, from first to second, was imperceptible. For how can that be verified, undergone in such a manner as to clear my name of all calumniating dust of labels that make it. at least in these parts. synonymous with heartless hingeless fabulation. It was always clear when the first dusk stopped and the second started. clear from the sky and the river below. and all it reluctantly reflected of a chaos in the highest branches from which. at last. a little calm. well-lit. was evicted. Suffice it to say the transition occurred somewhere between the going of the cows and the coming of the goats. On some days it seemed the significant moment was closer to the going than to the coming but there is no time now to investigate the wavering allegiance of that moment. First dusk was completely recapitulated in second so you did not have to notice comings and goings in the first dusk. in fact it was better if you were preoccupied with something else. a windlass or an anthill. for example. Then the recapitulation as something much more. far richer. than a repetition took you by surprise if not by storm. The transition between the second dusk and night was always depopulated of all ambiguity—in short. abrupt. It is safe to say night was born in the going of the goats. somehow ponderous as if with saddlebags along the ferny steeps. Descending they went on chewing with absolutely nothing to chew. unless you were so unmannerly as to assign them man's undiminishing cud of affliction. I was not unmannerly and so it is perhaps understandable that I found myself having to get away from dusk. first and second. second and first. the second from whose sentence inexact. rising and falling like an edict. there was no reprieve. A little warding off of the edict came with chanting but not enough. never enough. One night. every night. the sounds fell. the goats departed. I was left with myself. to myself. pregnant with vigilance yet supremely targetless.

Sleeping in a hut, I was comfortably on the margin of the forest, blue-black, and in the rain blue-green, and in the sun color of goat droppings. You might as well know I have given up trying to reckon with—capture, as the dilettantes say—its tone. Enthralled surrender to its shifts belongs to younger, though hardly better, days when I sought the dead in its every brake and copse. To end the matter I am willing to affirm the forest is the color of flesh. My dog, named Knut, lived placidly in the hut. He was placid because placidly capable of interring his cravings before I ever had to busy myself burying the evidence of his having satisfied them. When I returned from work he fetched me my slippers and my cracked spectacles from the low mantel, varnished by the waning sun. Though it waned the patches fibrillated. He tried upon occasion, did Knut, to fetch me the shadows on the sill—shadows of leaves and twigs feeble as leaves. He was an upright canine, correct in his bearing toward strangers when there were strangers come burlily to insist on an incontrovertible connection with our canine community, and skillful, with more tricks and less dolor, oh so much more skillful, in solitude. His tricks moved me to tears, the infrequent dolor left me completely cold. I thought I could hear, when he balanced himself on one toe, the not so far off flight of a flute, akin to sap striving upward in unblemished boughs. In short, his tricks pointed toward dolor, far more ingratiating than dolor outright. Visiting sometimes with neighboring families I wanted to believe they were happy, they believed they were, what with meals on time and the abundance at table. I could smell the soup a mile off. The man of the house was tall, gentle, bewildered by the attacks of his wife and daughters. He never replied, never fought back, for this was the way of the world. In my presence it was always the same daughter lashing out against him. Perhaps her tenacity in incising outburst was for my especial benefit, to impress upon me the depth and range of her joyless and uncompromising lucidity. She wanted above all to stave off my unworded verdict, the verdict of a stranger, harshest because most tempered.

After dinner they all sat around among their goats, on the back porch, looking up in the general direction of where I lived and deprecating without knowing they were mine the latest efforts at enhancing the forest's dour margin. Clearly that margin festooned with things that grow quivering as they grow usurped, from their blundering perspective, both the calm of the forest's deeps and the fattedness of the surrounding fields. Perhaps they wanted to believe there was a sharp demarcation between forest and fields and here was the margin aglitter making for a flagrantly gradual transition between them. The transition was an entity. Under the unfriendly smell of their gaze it became a clinical entity, a symptom fleshed out and achingly visible. Or perhaps enhancement of the margin put them gratingly in mind of a demarcation they wished to forget. Perhaps for as long as they could remember, should they wish to remember, the fields had been a continuation of the forest and the forest an extension of the fields, for in the rain wasn't the forest's blue green the white of the fields and at the onset of night wasn't the black and tiger red of the forest the spitting image of the field's pink and olive green. In their cavilling silence I could hear the lamentations at both forest and fields being called to a halt by the same wavering line of ragged bloom.

I never argued. listened only, the daughter continuing to attack the father as if that was still the only way to protect him from my merciless diagnosis. What did she know of the blur that alighted on my eyelids when I tried not to listen to her, she did not know it was a question not of hoarded lucidity but of escape, escape at all costs. But she went on believing—or rather. her vituperation went on believing—that humiliated he was no longer a target for the certainly greater venom I was storing within. Assailing she was rendering him impervious to the lance of my loquaciously damning gaze.

Sometimes I took her to town. There was never anyone when we arrived but when we were going back she found herself in full view of whole crowds begrudging the pout of her buttocks. We always ended up back in her room. almost bare. The few objects contained therein she overturned in passing. never understanding why she must try to destroy what promised continued faithful service, the subsequent gritting of teeth and thighs perhaps guessing that she was terrified of disappointment at some future time and so obliged to obliterate future time before its time. Once I attacked her. But nothing came of attack because I insisted on remaining on the margin of the forest of my cravings.

My cravings were out of place in such a place, that whence her gaze was fixed on my doings. I went back up into the forest and tore it to shreds. That tearing was an elegy on the temporary death of my cravings. Despite all my efforts to destroy it—in the way she went about destroying the few objects in her room?—the forest insisted on unearthing the scent of my cravings, or better yet its distant thunder unearthed the scent of their unspeakability When she spoke, at widely scattered intervals, trustingly the unspeakable welled up inside me. Her trustingness was ugly to me and not simply—not at all—because of its infrequency. In fact, the infrequency was a blessing. When I was assailed by the craving to touch her I was even more rapidly assailed by the craving to denounce her in every nook and cranny. At those times of unmitigated craving—mitigated only yet instantaneously by a countervailing craving—I had to move on, toward some forest phenomenon suddenly perplexing—more than perplexing, agonizing and agonizingly in need of decipherment. I did move on, that is to say away, far away, from her, from her likes, to the ostensibly ideal vantage whence perception and articulation of that perception were possible, that is to say, simultaneous—indistinguishable. Yet the closer I got the further it got. Proximity invariably dealt the death blow to this flight of blackbirds emerging from nowhere, that oracular fume above the gauzy treeline, this noise, that flash of brick-colored light. In the course of my dealings with her and with the progenitor she victimized the forest became not merely a hive of occult phenomena—occult until deciphered, meaning articulated—but the one place where I was outside myself at last, able to watch myself suffer.

Before bedtime they spoke most, always interrupting each other, and as one interrupted the other he (or she) stared straight into the eyes of the victim and the victim stared straight back. And all this gamesmanship was less a question of mutual reproach than of mutual bewilderment at what had just occurred, this joust of spoken thoughts overcoming other thoughts. Perhaps the collision of bewilderments could best be deciphered as a unison of resignation to spoken thoughts, thought words, as at best a temporary acquisition. Here they were, quarrelling on the back porch, about turkeys and fences and market prices, and yet now that it was all over once again nothing had been gained, nothing confirmed but the diabolical perdurability of phenomena, barely scorched by worded thoughts, perhaps softened a wee bit along their flinty contour before being sucked back into the old vat of unconceivability. Listening it became neither clearer nor more unclear whether words uttered as, in, thought impale phenomena or render them on the contrary more expertly elusive. Did the thoughts in fact cause the phenomena to fold back on themselves, invaginate into their opposite in defense against all this salivating hunger to fix, diagnose, impound for all eternity, so that what ultimately remained was neither the original phenomenon nor its opposite but a kind of unlocalizable shuttle among and between. I tried to shut my eyes and ears against the phenomenon under consideration. I told myself that the only phenomena worthy of decipherment were those forest-bred. Finally the father turned to me and brought the turkeys into my court. But I did not know how to talk turkeys.

Theirs was a new language and when I disembarked in one the first words I appropriated were despair, rapture, childhood. In them I had a foothold that, lodestonelike, drew many others into its lines of force. The women, unlike him, did not try to make me feel at home. Among them I had a sense of impenetrable intrigues, grievances as thick as the lentil stew they fed me. There was a pleasure too in making me feel it was solely on my account that

94

the half-audible incubation of these grievances had been temporarily abandoned. In short, the women undid me. There was no
possibility of recapturing myself in their shadow, all I was to
myself once again impervious to the annihilating echo of their
slavish tread. Sitting with the women I was too powerless, too
small, to invoke the filiations that might assist me in refuting
their claim that I was no more than a runt, a flea-bitten mutt
washed up on their muddy shores. There was no asserting my
connection with Knut, the low mantel on which my slippers lay,
the margin of the forest. I became what they wished me most to
be, an entity of the moment. My particularity was a colossal
affront and their presence depopulated me of all particularity, all
contouredness, all specific gravity. So reduced my only clues
concerning myself learned to come from their vicinity. Whenever
they deigned disdainfully to attribute to me a hut, a dog, a
pavemented kitchen garden I underwent for a moment the
excruciation of feeling myself beginning to exist anew. But all
these contortions were soon brought to a halt by a cough, a
sneer. And in any case and under the best of circumstances it
was excruciating to sit among them losing their thoughts, their
thinking words, to each other, wondering what was theirs to
retrieve, to call their own in the twilight of their days, after all
this shuttling of retaliatory confiscation. Perhaps they were
reconciled, had long before been reconciled, to a common stock
of thinking words, worded thoughts, shifting among, in the
spaces between, them.
I usually returned to my hut in the midst of the second dusk,
with the goats gambolling amidst the cows' leavings. I basked in
their gaze, a gaze that interrogated but wisely expected no
answers. That gaze generated questions but never in a million
years could it have coexisted along with the answers. I asked
myself if I shouldn't go down for good. I was surprised when she
appeared on the threshhold one night, at the beginning of the
second dusk, the first lingering inside me. She sat down and

began to speak, after every word a question mark, her speech was a play of shadow. Having made me a gift of her presence her presence now made it clear it could, would, promise me nothing. This was somehow satisfying, it was no longer a question of striving toward her. Suddenly it was only a questioning of listening and now that listening was not so difficult precisely because it was listening on behalf of another, the forest was that other. I did not try to make her say what would ultimately be acceptable to such a listener. I would never stoop to making her say what that listener must hear me repeating, report, if I wished to be seen in a plausible light. She had free rein. Knut licked her calves. She demanded that I come down, she wanted an answer quick, I could give none, I was now wedded to the future, already beating its stick along the gravel path leading to my front door —to my future report, verbatim, of all that was transpiring here. In spite of myself I went back with her. When I spoke to her and to her clan of the forest it was with a new, a positively apoplectic, urgency and they all hastened to cut me off before I could finish evoking what threatened, even now in its rudiments, to overwhelm, wash them away. Perhaps the forest was especially virulent because it had already begun storing her utterances, the pointed and precipitous remarks spewed out, serpentlike, in my hut. When I stopped speaking she turned away, ashamed of my submission. And it was just at this moment, enraged at her shame, that words came to me. But I was distrustful of these words, were they capable of painting a sentiment fully hatched— sentimental admixture of rage and pride—or were they trying to call a sentiment, any sentiment, into being, something to oppose to the monolithic thrust of her invidious recoil. Instead of speaking up, speaking back, I turned away. I wondered, turning, if the turning was itself the truest expression of my sentiment(s) or only an expedient deflection of, from, meaning still slumbering, still subjacent, surging turbulently but always in another plane, one inaccessible to the gasps of their prostration. Turning back

to them—to her—I felt I had undergone a change, I wanted to communicate the change, to assure her she was confronting a being different from the one sluggishly abandoned minutes before. But before I could celebrate I realized what was responsible for the change or rather for this suddenly clearly premature celebration of a change. I knew I was leaving, for good. Absence was already transforming her, into one the details of whose preposterous physiognomy no longer paralyzed the unwary onlooker. The bridge of her nose, the too large pores just above the pinched lips, the flawed iris, these no longer boded ill, no longer boded. I no longer demanded anything of them, I no longer interrogated them with a goatlike aversion to answers, I only asked and politely if they couldn't somehow manage to persist in their being somewhere out of my immediate vicinity. Hearing me announce my plans to go for good she asked, with the cruelty born of badly dissimulated panic, if I believed in it after all. The forest? The forest. I said it was never a question of belief but rather of the continuous upsurge of little tasks able to obliterate the need for belief. She shrugged as she had many times before. I could see she wanted me to take her with me, she was tired of the odors of a supper dish always plowed through far too slowly for her taste. I told her no, it wasn't possible. To be kind, or perhaps to be vicious, I added, At least not this trip. Abysses were fast springing up between us as we struggled now, we were both drawn by the scent but in the end found ourselves too finally sundered by wide water and the infinitesimal convulsions of its earth beneath.

Breadwinner's Ethic

Leaving the building he was completely unprepared for this quiet clarity of sunset after a by no means exceptionally cold winter day of flawed visibility. Above the apartment buildings the blue of dusk fading grew progressively thicker. Or rather, descending from the zenith the sky grew progressively more crystalline, barer, as if all of being, all its secrets and all impediments on the way to disclosure of those secrets were revealed to the bare bones at last. Among the bare bones, bones themselves, were a crescent moon and, some distance away, a single star taking it in tow. For a second, maybe a minute, as column upon column of headlights mounted at the red light, there was nothing separating him from a life ever so different from this. A life unencumbered with these details. Yet for this second, this minute, no detail was able to injure his dearly won yet distinctly, distinctively, affirmative communion with sky as all of being laid bare not only to his sight but almost to his touch. No detail—for example, those two red lights atop a fuliginous flue somewhere in the distance where billboards gave way to watertowers—could mar the purity of the deployed specimen, the sky as sea guiding him toward some atoll where misery and self-loathing as the spawn and plaything of crime in the streets and inept employers venting their frustrations at the drop of a hat did not exist. This dusk, this sky at dusk, this sky as dusk and dusk as sky, was the archetype of all dusks. For this moment and this moment only all times zones were equalized. It was dusk everywhere and anywhere. This moment, his, was everybody's, far and wide, plumbers and pedestrians, murderers and envoys. By the time he got to the end of the sidestreet taking him away from the core of the spectacle it was over, even on its margin. Blue's transparency as blue's opacity was over, done with. Pity, he knew, because that shortlived hue indulged his unavowable cravings as nothing else in being—reflected them back to him as something real yet undiagnosable. In its medium, on the playing field of its supreme mealleability, its supreme ... tolerance, he was permitted to relive youth's slow decay as a sum of parts each greater than the whole. He could smell the atoll's greenery.

Then he remembered his employers, the backbiting among his co-workers, the doltish irascibility of clients and potential clients. The rage began to mount. For a split second this was invigorating, to be opposed to all that was not he, not only the employers and the co-workers, but the chimneys smokily winking in feeble defiance of the dusk's unutterable statute, the derelicts conferring with their piss-stained topcoats between smeared explorations of trashcans filled, on streetcorners vertiginously desolate, to the brim. But by the time he reached the post office to drop the day's correspondence in the box he was no longer invigorated or rather it was no longer possible to let this invigoration proliferate unchecked. This invigoration was a trap. For wasn't rage what he was expected to do, couldn't this rage be immediately classified, bracketed, as the typical, the common, the all too predictable reaction under the circumstances. So this rage was no longer a challenge to all of being, big with opposedness—even the little postal box from connectedness to which he was having trouble disengaging himself was no longer cowering—but rather a dreary capitulation to being's all too flexible guidelines regarding organized opposition to run-of-the-mill flagrancies. Being had been hoping all along for just such an outbreak of righteous rage. Being believed that by all means he should grumble his way to a calmer view of things in just this manner. He was right to balk at

100

injustice. At the word injustice he could only laugh out loud.
The slot of the postal box seemed to chuckle along with him.

He thought of speaking to his wife. If he spoke of his rage he
knew she would listen politely, muffling her sombre excruciated
trepidation. In advance, he was amused and touched by this
deference to his incoherence. But he did not want to introduce
his rage into the home, where their baby might grow fretful and
afraid. He thought back to his own father's outbreaks of unmitigated despair and of how, at those times, the cold winter
night grew colder and the factory chimney across from the
humble dwelling rose up in surer-footed mockery of their thrift-
shop security. their poverty of plans.

He could not leave this job, not now, with alternatives too
perilously scarce. But how much longer could he endure her—
the employer's—whine incarnating, alas, the subtlest form of
offhand ingratiation of which she was capable and directed at
whomever she could find to carry out orders themselves a
lackey's paraphrase of incoherence from on higher.

He looked behind every time he saw a shadow encroaching on
his own, for this was a crime-ridden city with all the accoutre-
ments of an occupied one. He was surprised, over and over, to
discover that the shadow's substance was in fact a long distance
behind. He was slightly disappointed. After all, the sense of peril
at every hour of the day brought smouldering to fever pitch.

A few blocks away. he realized he had been weakly, dully
stumbling toward the mouth of the subway. The thought of
descending the steps and then, after the token slots, still another
set induced a suffocation that not even an unexpected gust from
the direction of Central Park could relieve. At the entrance the
same habitues of shadow were intoning their wares. Further
within, beyond the leafless trunks and the gas lamps, vehicles
were advancing at an unvarying rate of incessancy. The lamps
were the points of a lattice deployed to net these demons of the
night. It was as if both lamps and trunks had been implanted but

101

a minute or two before the next onrush to partition this chaos.
this chaos where none of the elements could be counted upon to
remain in place longer than the split second required for
recharging. It was only when he was across the street and
standing inside the doorway of a men's haberdashery forever
going out of business and forever marking down its prices on
hats. coats. sheepskin vests and corduroy jackets that the chaos
of moving vehicles seemed on the verge of domestication.

He tried not to think of individual cars. He thought of the
turnover. The notion of a constant turnover was something to
hang on to in these raw incautious times. So what if this or that
slimy scoundrel of an employer. this or that unbalanced street
being. was deciding it was well past his time to be thrown on the
slagheap of goods irreparably damaged. Didn't he participate in
a universal turnover. a flux very much vaster than himself yet
which deigned to partake of his flavor amid a myriad of other
flavors. a dimensionless heterogeneity that spoke for him better.
far better. than his delimited particularity ever could. He pursued
the thought not because it consoled but because its treacherous
quietism intrigued him. He wanted to see how long it could go on
laying a trap for his desperation. Though he did not spit or weep
or bang his fists against the store windows with their promise of
shoddily spectacular negotiation. something about his stance
had to be conspicuous because here. a secretary taking very tiny
steps against the blustering cold. and there. a fat balding
impresario in a garish pelt halted to light his cigar. were both
staring at him as one distinctly to be contemned and avoided.
Their look said. "Yes. You. Exactly what the tabloids and the
bland newscasters with their grin-infested faces and cardboard
camaraderie are always warning us against. I should have known
better than to come this way." It was as if he, Loophole. had led
them to this impasse. He joined the rush toward the subway
without conviction but with a sense that once within it would be
warmer and less bleak. He thought of going straight home and

102

before the festivities began listening to a favorite record—a Chopin nocturne, maybe, or the "Entr'acte Symphonique et Sommeil" from Tchaikowsky's "Sleeping Beauty"—but then he remembered the record player, like so much in the apartment, was defective. Every note of the piano was bound to be distorted, stretched out on the rack of a mysterious virulence. Perhaps it was better this way for what did the nocturnes do but exacerbate a feeling completely incompatible with what was demanded of him now and, to be fair, not by any particular individual, this or that vested scoundrel, but by the planet itself converging frowardly on the four horsemen.

He squinted into the distance just before going down under. Was that the name of the coffee shop across the way . . . The Four Horsemen. He looked up and around. It was as if the sky had actually grown dark and cloudy, not simply cloudy but cloudily purulent. Passersby were growing more ferocious in their sidelong glances. Wasn't that a police siren already littering Fifty-seventh Street with the bloody tatters of a nearby fray? Wasn't that hefty red stain somewhere between Fifty-fifth and Fifty-fourth a fire truck? Wasn't the world coming to an end at last. Wasn't the world, all of being, concentrated in, contracted to, the pinpint that was New York on New Year's Eve, about to succumb to the directives of the myth associating extreme violence with purgation and admission to a newer cleaner cycle, a cycle where what invoked prohibition in this world would come forth as bounteously exhorted. He wanted to lift up his arms in homage to whatever toothless ogre had concoc;ed of terminal festivity. "Welcome, very welcome indeed," he heard some Briton, presumably on holiday, utter to the prim and pinched companion that was, again presumably, his wife, the little woman, taken in tow like bloated moon by errant star and made to undergo the edifyingly rowdy splendors of Sodom. When he opened his eyes, not remembering having closed them, he saw that all was proceeding at its normal rate, nothing the

103

least bit excessive. Nothing the least bit symptomatic of imminent apocalypse. The four horsemen were clearly fast asleep on their steeds.

He could not bear to enter the subway. On the corner, where his favorite coffee shop was closed down for renovations, a florid-faced figure approached as if set down here, in this time and place, expressly to retort, "No apocalypse tonight, bub." Things were very much the same, that is as usual particularly refractory to accentuation much less premonitory exaggeration. Everything was sinking back into the woodwork, even the woodwork which, in this case, was a brittle amalgam of steel and celestial gas. For this New Year's Eve the furniture of being had vowed to be as inobtrusive, as plausible, as possible.

"Hi," said a voice. He turned. It was Lou Breckenbottom, toiler in the same office though not, thank Heaven, in the same cubicle. Lou looked miserable and clearly craved company. "Hi," Loophole replied, "Look," said Lou, "let me buy you a cup of coffee somewhere. I can't go home yet." There was a certain resonating truculence, as if a fibrous esophageal lining of fat, cigar smoke and tearful phlegm was being rent. "Sure, Lou," he said. They ended up very quickly in the coffee shop he had misread as The Four Horsemen. In fact, this was the Little Russian Tea Room, pitiful counterthrust to a fashionable monument just around the corner and adjacent to Carnegie Hall where—at this very moment—Alexis Weissenberg might be invoking Chopin's ghost. They took a booth near the window The waitress, looking bedraggled, almost sluttish, was already big with disaffection, the thinking slave's lot on New Year's Eve "Yes," she groaned. Lou ordered two coffees. When she was already out of earshot Lou cried, "And some Sweet 'n Low." He looked at Loophole as if he was an immigrant just washed ashore and said, "Sugar substitute. The wife always uses it. Makes a real stink if they don't bring it. Life is tough." This last, this zigzag into the general, filled Loophole with wonderment. But then Lou began to stare truculently down into the depths of the table top. This vigorous exercise of his speculative faculty had exhausted him. Lou no longer needed to talk, much less speculate on life's toughness. He needed a breathing body near his own, a lukewarm body. a bulk bulky enough to delimit somehow the divagations of his own despair. Loophole wanted to cry out wickedly, "I have no energy. I can't console you." But did Lou seek consolation? As bankrupt as the encounter now seemed, he relished this interval before it took definite form or ended definitively, before it succumbed to the regular rhythm of conversational give-and-take. before Lou. or he, or both of them them simultaneously, jumped for the first slim opportunity to gnaw off the same bone of grievance. Would Lou be the first to speak of their employer. As strained as the silence was becoming he did not want to shelve it alluding to the old charlatan and the whining consort Della. "So." Lou said finally. "What are you planning for tonight." "Oh." he replied. "nothing much." "What's nothing much." Lou blurted. There was hurt in his eyes, a certain imploring. It was as if Loophole's inscrutability was now reaching a kind of climax of intentional ill will. His look said, "I can't figure this guy out." "Nothing much" Loophole persisted. He, the wife and the kid. Jackie. age three years, were all going to the wife's sister's house in a fashionable part of lower Manhattan, where lofts pioneeringly converted to showplaces by enterprising young artists were now the residences of doctor-usurpers, lawyer-usurpers, accountant-usurpers.—all the refulgent little deities of the welfareless state. These. Loophole knew from experience. had the leisure to cultivate just the right nonconforming look for admission into the best cafes and galleries littering sidestreets and thoroughfares. The sister-in-law and her husband lived far more modestly but their aspirations were boundless. He. Loophole. was intent on their progress. the progress of their progress, with its vociferating ups and downs. For these two clearly did not derive much muddled mileage from the heavy-handed inscrutability he himself peddled. He was making it a practice to observe them with considerable interest, especially at those times when all seemed doomed, when exertion of any kind had all the farcical inconsequence of a hot air balloon's ascent.

He did not want to speak of the jaunt to lower Manhattan. He did not want to hear himself speaking of it, giving it shape, presence, certainty, irrevocability. Because it was still unclear that he would be going. Some contingency, some symptom of the planet's undoing, might intervene on his behalf. He wanted, this night above all others, to sink back on his bed, in the darkness and damp, as the sirens on the highway put his wretchedness to sleep. But he knew he would go, that he would have to go, for his wife's sake, for the sake of their child who was already avid of encounter.

Surprisingly, just before the coffee was set down along with the Sweet 'n Low—the waitress, for all her disaffection, was a true professional—it was he and not Lou who began to weep. He thought he could stifle the tears by blowing his nose and patting his eyes as if the light or the steam from his coffee was simply too much for his myopia. But Lou had clearly found him out and was deriving a certain pleasure from his pain. With the tears, dread and despair over his fate began to fade, not because they were in any degree played out, much less resolved, but rather because this implausible agglomeration of Lou and the light snow now falling without and the waitress retreating and the pastiness in the faces of the other customers who all looked like members of the same blighted family—this agglomeration was making him aware that he could endure at any one time, on any one occasion, only so much dread, so much despair, so much computation of future occasions for fear. For the time being, he was played out. And yet just as suddenly there was a dread of losing the dread and the despair. A carefully cultivated sense of dread was at all times a form of preparedness. As for those times when dread seemed especially uncalled-for—well, then, it could easily serve as a gratuitous penance magically annulling inevitable horrors to come through the flagrancy of its very gratuitousness. But did he still have the strength to persist in this invocational annulment of horrors sure to come. Could he parry the temptation of a little euphoria—induced, strangely enough, by the fluorescence overhead reducing all physiognomies to the same primeval paste—the way night watchmen parry the solicitations of sleep. He looked at Lou, sipping coffee from his spoon. The spoon did not look clean but Lou did not seem to care. Suddenly it did not seem right that he should be here, caught, compromised beyond appeal, labeled, diagnosed, straitjacketed away. But why. Simply because he had fallen into the trap of sitting down to a cup of coffee with a co-worker? He felt as if he had stumbled onto a land mine about to detonate as the snicker of his employer and his missus—as the snickers of all his tormentors, slovenly folk still unable to summate their particular and separate strategies into legitimately huddled conspiracy. No, he was left to wend his way among the discontinuities of their assailment.

"Sitting here," he said finally, "I feel the bosses are watching. It is as if we never escape them in any facet of our lives. It is as if our sitting here, sipping and chatting, is somehow reassuringly intelligible to their venality, their talent for sucking our blood. Is there any place where I am not a subsidiary of the bosses and their gang of inept slobs. It is as if every movement, every outburst, is already bracketed away long before it subsides. No way out, Lou. None. They're glad we're here. Working off our seditiousness, working off our rage, in such a constructive way." He felt Lou must warm to him or to the occasion he was creating through such a spasm of uncompromised spontaneity. He expected, in short, to be rewarded for such condescension to authenticity. It was as if all this fulfilled no need of his own but had been fabricated completely and utterly in deference to Lou's crying need for some kind of comradeship in mock-candor. But Lou retracted, looked as if he had just been assaulted. Clearly he preferred Loophole's inscrutability, seemed to long for it now. It was for his inscrutability, perhaps, that he had chosen Loophole as his coffee shop companion no matter how much he might seem to be butting his head against its refusal to budge an inch. But Loophole was already started and could not stop, not now, especially now that he saw the waitress, their waitress, being treated with impatient contempt by a boothed pair bearing a disquieting, a veritably appalling, resemblance to the boss and his missus. "I feel that anyone looking at us could say we have made peace with all that oppresses and that we accept our lot. I feel that Flatulong can see me from afar and that he has typed and bracketed me away." "So what do we do," Lou asked, as if they were two gobs out for a night on the town. "Never give way to sitting in coffee shops." Loophole answered, with his eye hard on Flatulong's *susie* a few tables away.

"Never do anything that can be labeled, typecast, taken as proof of capitulation." "To what." Lou cawed. "To being." "To being what." He was opening one of the packets of Sweet 'n Low. Loophole looked around. He did not want to be more specific, less zigzaggingly general. "To being a maggot on the shitheap," he said finally, and with immense satisfaction for in capitulating to Lou's need for specificity he had transcended the murkiness of his invocation. Such crude directness must surely win Lou's grateful attentiveness. But Lou looked repelled instead of grateful, as if he had violated a very clear-cut image of himself ' that Lou had been doing his utmost to safeguard. Loophole felt furious at feeling remorseful.

Lou looked at him frightened by his own disgust. But then there was a subtle but unmistakable shift in the key of his retraction. It was as if Lou had placed him at last. His features seemed to rejoice with a kind of soggy-eyed security, still truculent. Their stares collided then went separate ways, parallel into perdition it seemed to Loophole. Loophole was afraid to move. For every moment would necessarily be referred back. But where? To his roots in, connectedness with, his tribe. To the always too

108

conspicuous exertions of his tribe, its flagrancies very much alive, very much rekindled in him, in his oratory serving only to provoke dissatisfaction, irremediable unappeasable discontent. His kind was always stirring up trouble, inveighing against the Flatulongs of the world. Wasn't his kind always to be found down through history implicated in some form of atrocity or other. What matter in what capacity they served as the knives emerged from their sheaths, whether as victims or perpetrators In any case they brought out the worse in their fellow men. Yes, he. Loophole, could almost smell the wary weary peasant sophistry at work in Lou's entrails. It was only because of Loophole's hysteria and capacity for exaggeration thta things were going awry this evening. Lou's eyes seemed to say, Nothing is awry except what you imply and more than imply is awry. Finally Lou said, "Your tribe, forced to live in exile on the periphery of things, of . . . being, has always tried to lure others—supremely content to paddle down the mainstream—to their extremity. Oh why has its talents never been content to remain commensurate with its numbers. Eh? Why must it be always straining for this major impact out of all proportion." "Out of all proportion to what?" Loophole cried. "To the world as you wish it to be, as you want to believe it is?"Loophole, hearing himself shriek and seeing all these faces turned toward him, did not know what to do, where to go. At the same time he wished to strangle Lou right then and there for forcing him to commit the sin of . . conspicuousness. "You don't belong anywhere," Lou muttered. "Why did Flatulong take you in in the first place. I wonder." "I'm guilty, in other words," said Loophole. "But of what. Of having been, through my forbears, a repeated target in the past," He threw what remained of his coffee in Lou's face. He had no fear. He knew, somehow, that the coffee was cooler than tepid. Just when he was beginning to feel sufficiently fortified to depart at last, holding back only from fear of crime on the streets and the sight of the destitute and deformed with whom he felt too

109

much of a kinship at this moment. Loophole noticed that Lou's snivelling truculence was gone, and had been replaced by a certain slyness, as if in refusal to say all. Was he saying all when he finally broke forth with, "Want to come to a party tonight?" He did not answer at first, fidgeted, instead, with his gloves that were soaked through and through though he could not tell why. "What's holding you back?" He was surprised, even wounded, by Lou's saying this, as if all this fidgeting could easily be bracketed as a holding back. It was as if Lou knew him too thoroughly. Had he been in fact bracketed and diagnosed away by this peasant long before. And all along thinking it was he who had the upper hand. He had even been a little bored by his mastery over the situation with its obvious absence of the titillating element of occasional surprise attack. "You're so silent," Lou said. He did not answer. He went on being silent. He intended to remain silent as long as the situation could stand it. Lou waited. He continued to sip his coffee. He clearly did not reproach Loophole for having had to wipe off his face and shirtfront. He was clearly not intimidated. Finally he said, "So what have you decided." It was immediately obvious that silence was no longer giving him an edge. Had it ever given him an edge, though? Lou was holding up this silence, this mastery of silence, between two fingers. Then he tossed it away as he might have tossed away a flake of skull, or a rodent audacious enought to have invaded the aged rents of a prize ottoman. Silence was no longer a weapon or rather its function as weaponry was being temporarily shelved. Some time ago—but when, when—silence had ceased to be the vehicle for transcendence of intelligibility to one's fellow men, and had undergone demotion into the merest refusal of self-defense, everybody's birthright. Lou had blithely—as only the rudest natures can, Loophole knew, those natures for whom the world was their unequivocal unequivocating oyster —bypassed whatever menace had been latent in his silence in order to bear down upon it as fact, as the lowliest of datums proving that Loophole was not only intelligible but a scared rabbit, to boot. All this time he had been trying to constrict himself to a smaller and smaller pinpoint of inaccessibility, a subtler and subtler knot repudiating all commonness, all sign and symptom of the already known, the bracketable. Yet what did this striving amount to now in the retrospect inflicted by Lou's invincibility but a shrill well-nigh hysterical craving to elude a world without nuance in whose eyes he was already a captive. What did the Soviet troops marching into Afghanistan care, for example, about this fatuously stouthearted refusal to stoop to intelligibility. Here was Lou telling him he was intelligible, all too intelligible. Or rather Lou had found a way to make him intelligible, to deform his striving into what could pass, all too easily, for the fall into classifiable typehood. He loathed Lou. The best end-of-season gift anybody could give him at this point would be to see Lou lowered into boiling oil. He, for one, would not flinch from the vivacity of the death spasms. "Come along, come along," said Lou, holding up the face of his watch to the fluorescence as if it were a family photograph Loophole had just handed him. "But," said Loophole. "Can't you phone your wife." He did not know how to respond. All he could think about was his brother-in-law and sister-in-law. It was a tradition—how he loathed the word—for the four of them to spend New Year's Eve together. If he went with Lou he would forfeit the brother-in-law's tormenting of the sister-in-law. Then, a little after midnight, he, the brother-in-law, would come round and confess before all those assembled, friends, relatives and besotted acquaintances, that he loved and needed her, that her patience was exemplary, how did she go on tolerating him. And he, Loophole, standing near the window and looking out over the city, over the snow-covered rooftops if there was snow, would pretend not to be hearing over his absorption. And so adept was he at hearing without seeming to hear, so rabid and yet so reserved was his curiosity, that everyone always took him for the one guest who

111

simply did not care, was too much situated elsewhere to care But he did care, wondering what compelled the making of amends. What caused the homeostatic click back to amends-making in the mechanism pain kept so well-oiled. "My brother-in-law and his wife have invited us. My wife's sister." How could he explain to Lou that he had no way of assuring himself it was New Year's Eve if the pair were not present. Their presence permitted him to compare the evening's muscle tone with that of evenings past and, once satisfied by the approximate sameness of the measurements, feel that the evening had been indubitably undergone. Their presence would make whatever might be experienced tonight verifiable as authentic lived experience since its undulations were easily enough calibrated against what was already bracketed, fossilized as lived experience, "Get your coat," Lou said, picking up the check. He could not remember the waitress having brought it. He sank back. It did not seem as if he would be able to rise to any occasion. "What kind of party is it supposed to be?" he asked, once they were outside. It had turned colder. The hotels along Seventh were in the midst of early evening activity. Tourists looked out at him and Lou dutifully, between gulps, as if they were very much part and parcel of a landscape that must be dutifully memorized for the folks back home. Yet these tourists did not seem to quite believe in him as they believed, for example, in the taxis parked at the curb in front of the revolving doors. He, Loophole, was obviously not extreme enough or extreme enough in a way that ws susceptible to some kind of quick caption, some kind of ingenuous, rapturously disapproving verdict. "A lot of interesting people," Lou said, "I should call my wife." "She can come too." He was no longer thinking about what he was saying, he seemed completely caught up in the pavement's play of light and shadow and in the innumerable transactions that were coming to birth and dying. This was Lou's element. His very stride strove to say that no longer trammeled by office duties and intrigues this was a new, the real, Lou. The stride said that Lou expected Loophole to take a back seat, to follow dutifully behind his mentor, become a kind of ambulatory almsbox into which Lou might, at his leisure and as warranted by the rhythm of their irrepressible upsurge, discharge a few of his most telling—because most starkly uncharitable— observations on life, love and death. But not work, not work, tonight. Loophole struggled to walk beside him as an equal but no matter what stride he assumed he always felt like a satellite. It was as if every stride had been spewed forth from Lou's center of gravity as unusable and foisted off on his ataxia. In short, he, Loophole, felt as if he was actually inhabiting or inhabited by Lou's least enviable attributes, trying them on and out for size on Seventh Avenue of all places, and on New Year's Eve no less. They passed a tobacconist. Cigarette pack wrappers from around the world were glued to the window. They provoked, in Loophole, a hunger for faraway places, for the greenery of his dusky atoll. Assuming Lou was incapable of such a hunger he felt he was escaping him at last, at least for a moment. "Want a cigar," Lou said. "Oh no, that's right, you don't smoke." How had Lou—talking not so much to as past him—come to this conclusion. But suddenly, horrifyingly, it did not matter whether or not the conclusion applied. It did not matter if Lou did not see him for what he was, blithely attributed tastes and affinities that did not in the least fit. All the same Loophole felt pinned down, impaled, suffocated. Inaccuracy was as potent an implement of impalement as accuracy.

He was located, so what if some distance to the right or left of where he believed himself to be. He would simply have to twist and contort himself into the serene embodiment of all that was subtended by Lou's misconception. At a red light, Lou looked at him with wizened foxiness and asked, at the same time nudging him lightly in the ribs, "So what is it. Can't you tear yourself away from your brother-in-law?" "I didn't say I liked him. But I am inexplicably drawn to what we can call, for brevity's sake, his antics. They place me." He shook his head at himself. As they crossed over he became aware that though he writhed under the glass of Lou's misconceptions—this placement against which there was no appeal—still he craved some other kind of placement. But was this other kind a kind of placement. He talked quickly to clarify more for his own benefit than for Lou's. "When he behaves in so reprehensible a manner, holding back not only from his wife but from the humor which is native to his temperament and his only source of charm, he seems to be sparing me from so disastrous a course. Even if the day before I have behaved in exactly the same manner—allowing for one or two slight variations, of course—it seems as if he has erected the whole situation, the whole performance, for no other purpose than to prove that for all the similarity of my own miserable frustrations, I am very different. His crimes of the heart not only deform my past crimes into a form totally different from his but sketch a future of abstention from these crimes if I wish to feel righteous and worthy and I do.

"In relation to his, my past crimes are suddenly minor, venial, laughable. Following the curve of his hopelessness, his despair, his all too human pusillanimous inability to accept life's gall without blaming somebody else—in this case his sublime and blameless helpmate—it is as if I have traced the extinction of my own. This will never happen to me though in fact this is always what is happening to me. Nevertheless consigned to the periphery of his conspicuous frailty, I feel light as a feather, free as a bird. For I am not he. I have been spared his noxious intelligibility to clicking tongues. Fixed and formulated, he has backed himself up against a wall to serve as example of that to which one is reduced when one's impotence in the face of circumstances becomes too . . . vociferous. For a split second I feel infinitely strong relative to his self-expenditure. It is as if he has sucked up and spewed forth into that self-expenditure all the latent tendency that would lead me to perform as he did, as he does, as he is bound to do again. Placing himself he has permitted me to place myself nowhere. So," he concluded. with a certain relief. "I am unlocalizable." He turned to Lou and added. "And you. old Lou. want to deprive me of that signpost in the blizzard." Lou sounded. as he said. "No sign of rain or snow." as if he was chewing on a wad of caramel. When they were well past the Americana and well into the tinsel of Times Square Lou turned to him and said. "So the fact he has let himself go. become the victim of your . . . looking and listening. becomes an occasion for rejoicing. Things all of a sudden don't look quite so bad for you. His kind of tantrum is there in reserve should things ever become intolerable. But things may never become intolerable precisely because you know how to skirt the guideposts incarnated by his tantrums. Feeling superior to him for having given way. expended himself. feeling superior to him as all of being making a disjointed and scandalous spectacle of its blustering impotence—feeling so goes a long way toward attenuating the intolerability that would. under ordinary circumstances. lead you to bite into the reserve his indiscretion has circumscribed. Things are looking up." Lou looked to the scintillating billboards as if they were taking his ironic prophecy a bit too literally. "You brother-in-law has done the worst and is still here to tell the tale. And look at you. You have held back. You haven't like him done your worst. Surely some kind of reward is in store for your mammoth abstention from such flagrancies." In spite of himself. Loophole's tongue was hanging out anticipating the reward. "Your reward." Lou guffawed. "is the party I'm taking you to."

Lou suggested, since they had plenty of time. that they stop in one of the pinball parlors. Before he could express his disinterest, Lou had shouldered him within. He stood to one side of Lou's jerky exertions. and heard him say above the clash of the balls, "In other words, this brother-in-law, what did you say his name is. rehabilitates you of an infirmity you didn't even know you had until you watched him perform—but which you may very well have and toward whose crisis points you may at this very moment be moving at incredibly high speeds. I don't think, Loophole, you can steer clear of this infirmity forever, no matter how blatantly painted the guideposts shooing you off and away. Desire will overtake you ultimately." "Stupid!" Loophole cried. "Desire has never been a stumbling block. I can purge myself of desire in a minute if it means that I avoid bracketing, being nailed to the wall, diagnosed into a straitjacket and forgotten." Lou merely shrugged, as if at bombast. The game was far more intriguing than Loophole's protestations. "I'll never be like my brother-in-law," Loophole persisted, a little sulky. But he could not squelch the sulkiness. "He sounds like an unmitigated failure," Lou ventured absent-mindedly. He was fishing for coins in the pocket of his trousers. "That's precisely what he is not," Loophole intoned, grateful for this opening. "He is one of those failures whose failure abuts, in fact, on success, is always very much in the vicinity of success. And there is the ignominy. That he is not quite good enough rather than completely, refreshingly unacceptable, unfit beyond appeal." Enumerating this unmitigated failure, Loophole felt himself very close to the euphoria induced a short time before, had it been only a short time before though, by the palpitation of the sinking azure. But Lou did not seem impressed with, had perhaps not even heard one syllable of, this sidestepping paean to himself.

In revenge, Loophole said, "I can't come to the party. They're expecting me." Lou looked at him as if he were a child and said, "Now look. They're perfectly capable of taking care of themselves. Such a worry wart." And once again he felt that Lou did not know him at all and that once again he would be forced to twist and contort his being into compatibility with what was sketched in Lou's little outburst. It was as if whatever came out of Lou's mouth must be understood as having nothing to do with him, Loophole, as he wished to be seen, if he indeed ever wished to be seen, but rather with whatever platitudinousness was near at

116

hand to most plausibly fit a situation completely beyond his, Lou's, grasp. yet of which he, Lou, must always end up master. He made the wound comply with the contour of the shrivelled bandage popping out of his sidepocket. "Let's go," said Lou, leading him out of the pinball parlor. This comradely insistence was, Loophole was sure, very much in the service of humiliating retaliation. But then, when they were nearing Macy's, he felt he had imagined everything, that Lou had, in fact, a vigorous respect for his being. They sat down in Herald Square. The pigeons kept away. He kept telling himself they were mad, quite mad, to be sitting here, easy prey for the criminal element scattered over the face of the city. But Lou would not budge. By ten o'clock they had reached a deserted street between Ninth and Tenth Avenues. A pallor of imminent rain hung over the row of houses. Several times as they walked along Lou said, "This is it." But whatever he said seemed, as they advanced, more and more to have been said at random with no particular house, no particular street even, in mind, though this, the one they were now traversing, had unleashed a certain unfamiliar playfulness in Lou's lilt. Looking up, he saw a head appear at one of the windows of a bland and effaced-looking brownstone. It belonged to a woman, an expectant woman. She waved though Lou did not notice. Without noticing, however, he began to mount the steps leading to the double doors, their lintel festooned with tender gargoyles.
A lace curtain with a tame little tassel hung almost to ground level yet allowed for discernment of the stairwell's onset, red-carpeted and impeccably clean. He followed. Lou opened the door and climbed. Loophole detected laughter not far off and smelled hot pot pies and other specialties of this wet season. He called out, "I must call my wife." but Lou, looking drugged, did not answer. There was a vast lumbering exuberance in all his movements. The reek of the cooking made Loophole in a way glad that his wife was not here to observe how quickly he was

117

sinking. "I have no choice," He told himself. "I have to follow."
The door of an apartment on the third floor was opened by a
woman, presumably she who had gesticulated so violently behind
the pane. Looking back and down, he saw an old woman huddled
in shawl and skullcap looking up with displeasure from the
landing below. Was it myopia lending her curiosity—and a
genial curiosity at that—this look of taut irascibility.
One inside he began to shiver. There was no heat and the
cooking furnished the surroundings with little warmth. "Here,
on my right," cried a voice. He looked to Lou to see if he would
react but his companion seemed very much engaged with the woman
who had opened the door. She was rattling on about taxis and
the difficulty of making them stop late at night and the murder of
a close friend out in Brooklyn on her way back from a concert
when all of a sudden . . . He realized the voice had been speaking
to him and that he was expected—the guests were watching,
judging him with the murderous neutrality that sweeps through
members of a group whenever the solitariness of a new recruit
invents their contrasting cohesion—to sit down. He recognized
another co-worker in the group. This co-worker gave no sign of
recognition.
Perhaps this co-worker was paying him back for having always
been made to feel that even the slenderest exertion of amenity
toward the boss, toward Flatulong, was collusive treachery of
the basest sort. Before Loophole could speculate further he
almost fell over seeing Flatulong emerge from what had to be the
kitchen. Its window gave on a brick wall that couldn't be more
than a foot away. Chill and suffocation fought for a foothold
though he had none to give at this moment. Flatulong looked
him straight in the eye and incipient hilarity gave a slightly
different tilt to his preposterous features. Laughing in a manner
that was not all that distinguishable from crying, Flatulong
passed on.
Those seated in a circle, some on chairs, some on cushions, were

118

neither friendly nor unfriendly. If they did not exaggerate the anomalousness of his presence neither did they make any effort to welcome him. Were they revolted and fatigued by what they perceived as an eagerness to participate at all costs. At that moment he needed most of all to find a toilet. Lou was standing in a corner of the room near a fireplace that did not work too well, still chatting. Looking around, he observed that Flatulong was talking to Mrs. Flatulong in a small room. With alarm, he realized this was the toilet and that they were consequently blocking his passage. Every so often she looked in his direction. What was her name in fact. Greta, Delilee Mae? Was her maiden name Gilhooley as all her underlings insisted. There was fear and contempt—a contempt still flexing its wings yet proleptically attuned to danger from his direction. There was news for him. Of this Loophole was sure. Information she had to convey from her chief, new ideas that were sure to be good for business. Was she making every effort to memorize all he had irascibly spewed forth a short time before in the office. Whenever he tried to catch her eye she looked away. He no longer felt the need to call his wife because what was this party after all but an excruciated prolongation of the work week.

Flatulong and the missus emerged at last from the toilet. Abandoning her at once he advanced on a company of prosperous-looking simians and proceeded to bemoan the losses incurred as a result of the immeasurable incompetence of the hired hands working out of the Manhattan office. For this pair kept more than one office. There was, for example, the shingle in Leche-Mon-Cul, Indiana and the suite in Doltville, Vermont. The simians shook their heads sadly if asynchronously, as if they understood. They too had their problems with the insubordination and poor work attitudes of assorted fellahs. So, Loophole thought, this is what my rage reduces to in the end—insubordination. Before insubordination was conflagrant it was already strait-jacketed. He could no longer bear to look Gilhooley's way. She

119

seemed to emit a visible stench. Every now and then Flatulong looked over at her. perhaps to see if she was on the verge of carrying out his instructions. Though she pretended to be immersed in what the person before her was saying she was in fact aware of every one of these looks. The person before her seemed to be appealing to her. woman to woman. rawly and nakedly. Gilhooley was looking conspicuously strong and superior in her refusal to yield. Given her infinite capacity for self-suppression in the face of her lord and master's raucous waspish demands why should anyone else have the right to rise up and proclaim crude misery to be anything more than insignificant.

He sat down on a cushion and felt his stomach churning. He could not understand why it should be churning now that he had located his, its, target of torment. With Gilhooley so near. with whatever issue she had dragged along with her so obviously near resolution, why should he continue to torment himself. He watched her move across the room. He looked around to see if the other guests might be undergoing the same unspeakable revulsion. But they seemed to take her bovine canter very much in stride. Some even waved as she passed. And at each wave. Flatulong, very much oblivious to his wife except as an errand boy, turned grinningly to the waver as if it was he who had just been personally complimented. as if all credit for this charm and grace he, for one. doggedly refused to perceive. must accrue to him.

For a moment or two. as Loophole watched the guests express individually their admiration and affability. he could almost feel he was losing his grip on rage. on disgust. This affability was telling him it was all right, perfectly all right. not to loathe her so ferociously and that he was very much entitled to celebrate. quietly, a sabbath from this penal servitude of loathing. And that he would in no way metamorphose into the most loathsome _ of men relinquishing his grip on the loathing of one who deserved to be loathed above and more relentlessly than all others. In short, he would not be less of a man loathing her less. But what did these nondescripts know of her and of his burden of loathing. Theirs was only a casual relationship.

A guest who looked mightily like Lou advanced toward him. He did not see anything unseemly in settling himself on the same cushion. They were in the same room, invited by the same hostess. Therefore, they had every reason to consider themselves lifelong buddies. "So what do you do," said this cheerful and forthright comrade. He could not bear to answer. Mightn't this be one of Lou's decoys and wasn't Lou, after all, a decoy sent forth by Flatulong. Before he could answer, the comrade said, "My name is Al. I work for that guy over there." But he did not point, as if he would have been pleased to have any one among that swarm of dewlapped worthies for a boss. "So what line are you in?" Al asked. Again, before he could answer, "Do you like your branch of the operation." Screwing up his face as if stumbling his way toward a point of view completely new to him Loophole said, "I used to like it. I mean I used to have the time to think about what I really wanted to be doing instead of that. But even after I had finished off the few little tasks assigned me by Flatulong and his slut I was still not happy. I kept wondering why all this melancholy in the midst of the suddenly plenteous void where my time was, at last, very much my own." Al looked unnerved. He was turning in all directions at once. "Time to think? time very much your own?" Al was appalled. Loophole felt dizzily absurd giving away his secrets. What if Al gave him away and the Flatulongs descended upon him thrashingly. "You see," he resumed, throwing all caution to the wind and as if cuddling up to Al, who—this had to be said for him—did not edge away or flinch, "even when there is the prospect of my own time it leaves a sour taste. I see now that what I want, what I have wanted all along, is a certain kind of recognition, out in the open. I have this hunger to be perceived—and by Flatulong and the missus of all people—according to my own perception of my

121

merits. And what makes it worse, these merits are indissolubly bound up with a staunch repudiation of the work they foist off on me. And this impossible state of affairs is destroying me, eating away at me." It pleased him to see Al growing more and more uncomfortable, more and more filled with a rage of incomprehension streaked with dread-laden glimmers. To prolong the discomfort, Loophole repeated his observations concerning this sick need for recognition. "And I know it's no good," he added. Al looked up as if they were at last penetrating to the heart of the matter. "It's never any good," Al stated, "to look for a way out of loyalty. One has—you have—an obligation to do the very best job you can." Enunciation of his creed irradiated Al's beefy features. He became a seraph stationed before the imposing portals of the job market. He superintended the turnover. Loophole noticed that many of these folk were young but men and woman of means nonetheless, tastefully attired and publishing ever so tastefully their creditable exertions in the name of profit and loss.

"It's no good because it keeps me, this hunger, from doing what is really important. It is destructive, not to the work I perform for Flatulong, which never takes more than a few minutes, a few mindless minutes, but to any serious thought about my own work, the work I may someday do, the work I may someday be able to oppose to all this flurrying inconsequence that justifies my weekly paycheck. Not that when I do have time for myself, time to think about what I might one day do, it isn't a mixed blessing. Having such time for myself, I am mercilessly exposed to the most sinewy and oppressive problems of my . . . being. And they become most sinewy and glaring when there is no possibility of being distracted away from them by the conveniently oppressive imposition of tasks from without, alien tasks, tasks that perpetuate the fatuities of Flatulong and Sons. So it is precisely at those moments when I am left most alone, a forgotten underling as it were, that I most rage at my employers. And yet at the first sign of their reappearance I am even more excruciated. I cannot bear to have them to descend upon me when I can flaunt absolutely no connection to authentically frenzied thought about the work to come, the real work, the true work. When I am doing absolutely nothing with my free time, dearly won, I brook interruption least gracefully. They have caught me in the act of having no act to call my own, as it were." "So," Al intoned, "you are most enraged at alien tasks imposed when there is no prior connectedness of your own to stand in the way of your performing them." On the verge of tears, Loophole affirmed, "I am most afraid of being lured away when there is nothing to be lured from, except a latency. In the intervals between the blood, sweat and tears inseparable from concentrated thought about the true work, the future work, the work I can call my own, no true work exists. And I, in consequence, do not exist except to be called away into decomposition at the hands of puffy alien projects. And what are these projects, these tasks, but their stratagems for keeping me far from myself." For a split second he felt that Al's beefily irradiated features understood his rage. But then Al shrugged off this understanding which made him hot around the collar. He began to lick his lips and shift his weight from one flabby buttock to another on the cushion, sagging, now, appreciably. It was somehow a point of honor not to understand, to understand as little as possible, incomprehension was, in this case, inseparable from manly integrity, and from manly tenacity held in reserve for the tasks to come. A gruff and fidgeting incomprehension was, Loophole could see, a declaration of stouthearted innocence, virile and seraphic. This constructed inability to understand was Al's pat on Al's own back, a warning that love of work, love of bosses, love of subjection, was not as natural as he had up to now needed to believe—a warning in the form of that pat. The pat retightened the tenuous grip on workerly loyalty. "I love my work," Al said, watching Flatulong nibble from Gilhooley's well-stocked plate. As the spouse ingested,

Gilhooley looked at and then beyond, far beyond, him with a smile of insipid and ravished contentment as if the most beautiful thing on God's earth—this coy connubial partaking—had been achieved. She looked beyond, far beyond, petty imputations of delight at the jealousy their bliss must be inducing. Flatulong, his mouth full and a beringed forefinger digging into the space between back teeth, lifted his head from the vicinity of the plate to guffaw, though no one had spoken. Looking straight at the pair, Loophole said to Al, "Even if it is work for others, on behalf of already fatted cows, serving to enrich only the exploiter, even if the very natural need to create for oneself can expand only in the domain of his unyielding rapacity. Even if you can reproduce yourself only in the image of your oppressor." "Hey, now hold on a minute," Al crooned. He bristled, he was on the verge of getting up off the cushion to fume in full face rather than continue wincing in bloated profile. "You have to think of it from the boss's point of view." He wanted to push Al off the cushion rather than wait for him to rise to the full height of his outrage. But he felt that any gesture, however forthright, however necessary, would only endanger him, render him visible, intelligible, diagnosable. "Your work attitude is bad." Al said. Was Al speaking a little too loudly in order to alert the Flatulongs to the traitor in their midst. "Work attitude." Loophole muttered, looking up now to Al at his full height, "that is what is so unbearable. One is thrown scraps and one is still required to cultivate and maintain in the face of all impediments a good work attitude. So the workaday world is nothing more than a prorogation of those grade school sessions where only the slimiest pupil, the most subservient and constricted, can hope to wrest the puniest of encomiums from between the parched pursed lips—superior and inferior—of the presiding pedagogue." Before Al could protest, or tear the few remaining hairs out of his pate. Loophole was off on a different track. "When they foist some absurd assignment off on me—some task which is so obviously

124

useless except as a tactic for keeping me busy—then I become terrified of being unable to return to thought about the true work. I am afraid that even this lowliest of exercises will incapacitate me for whatever it is I was put on earth to do. I don't want to be cancelled out before my time." "So," said Al, looking crafty yet oddly compassionate, "it is as if their slovenly exploitative whining has some deep malevolent intent—to cut you off from all communion, all connectedness, with your deepest parts. And yet, if I read you right, when you are idle, when you don't know how to dispose of the little freedom that sometimes falls to your lot, you are the first to invoke just such malevolence, just such mutilation."

They were now both staring toward Lou. As they waited for him to join them—he seemed several times on the verge of concluding his conversation with a fat three-piece-suited hearty but was always drawn back, there was always some point about this best of all possible profitable worlds that required clarification or some mutual congratulation that demanded a more forceful, a more blatantly emphatic. reprise—Loophole observed that Al was genuinely mortified. He began to pout, to whimper like a little child. "Hell," he chanted flabbily, "you tell me they give you time—" "Unwittingly," Loophole reminded. "What do you want. They allow you to, so to speak. eat them out of house and home. And here you are complaining." Loophole's confidences were proving. in their leisurely echo, to be too much for Al to bear. "Yes," Loophole cried—his intensity multiplied manifold by impatience at Lou's loitering—"I have the freedom now and then to . . . think about the true work. But every free moment always turns out to be the wrong moment. Every free moment I cave in. These opportunities are always nothing in themselves, merely the sign of all those future opportunities certain never to materialize in time to coincide with the upsurges, few and far between, of desire. As for the scraps of opportunity thrown to me now, they are as good as useless for I can never summon forth enough desire to exploit them." Al shrugged as if to say, Whose fault is all this mess but your own. Hearing the word "exploit", Gilhooley was already bearing down upon them, already forming her lips to whine the utterance of his name. Should he tell her, he wondered, this was not office hours, ma'am.

Loophole just stood there as she advanced on them, lumbering, graceless, rendered even more graceless by this farcical effort to appear very much in her element among these successful folks enjoying a rare leisure moment supersaturated with the farts and belches of their own kind only. The urge to kill was overcoming him again. It was as if this graceless clucking tread was devised especially—exclusively—to torment him. As she got closer, steering her way past innocent bystanders, her tottering arrogance seemed more and more to be doing away with him, with his essential being, consigning him to a point on the horizon whence retrieval would be easy enough when she was ready to have him once again at her beck and call. "Mr. Flatulong was thinking," she whiningly began, converging on that far point: She tried to transform into something improvised and whimsical this be-draggled delivery of somebody else's—in this case her lord and master's—instructions. Or if she was making no pretense of being anything but a messenger she at least tried to sound as if she more than heartily concurred in all she was at liberty to paraphrase. But at the bottom of this brew of sounds—braying, garbled, cracked and phlegm-coated sounds—was the rabid eagerness to do her duty, to follow her instructions to the letter. Loophole waited with rage in his soul as he watched her formulate the thoughts of another. Behind them, not in the toilet this time, but in the damp constricted kitchen, one of the female guests, who from her stance obviously considered herself an attractive, a daringly attractive specimen of prosperous aggressivity out there in the arena of debentures and escrow accounts, was placing a pastry plundered from the low table near the fireplace into her lover's mouth. He, tending to stoutness, had the same air of buoyant, of elected, prosperity. To Loophole, sweating in the shadow of his employer's flunkey, there was something simply unbearable in this little life-affirming tableau unfolding for the benefit of some gullible bystander. He refused to be straitjacketed into the role of bystander, armpits damp with awe at the sight of such opulent effervescence. Turning away only brought him face to face, once again, with Mrs. Flatulong. "So when am I supposed to start work on this assignment," he asked, stonefaced. Al, who was still beside him and appeared very much impressed with what Gilhooley Flatulong was trying to pass off as fluttery expertise, now looked at him with a mixture of vindictive pleasure (So, you son of a bitch, now you'll have to start buckling down and get cracking) and nervous anticipation (Does this dear sweet little lady know just how seditious is he to whom she is delegating all this responsibility?). But beneath the stonefacedness was terror. Less and less was she recognizing him for what he knew himself to be. And what did he know himself to be. Desperately he wanted to point to the porous dusk above the chimneys that was no longer. His being was inextricably bound up with the being of that dusk. But that dusk was no longer. Its being was no longer. He, by extension, had no being to recognize. She was right then to bypass him in the name of the urgency of her instructions. "Now," Gilhooley replied, with unmistakable irritation in her voice. But the irritation was somehow not large enough to elicit from him an opposing irritation. "But I'm on my own time now," he told her. She shrugged, hand on hip, and sucked air through her teeth as if to say, Only the lowliest of the low would stoop to recruit such lame excuses for their hebetude. She did say, "Mr. Flatulong never stops thinking," with a certain sneer. "What," he said bluntly, with the directness of frenzied rage barely reined in. But before she could answer Flatulong was calling her over. At the sound of his voice she became completely oblivious to everyone and everything. When she was gone, Al looked at him smilingly and said, "Time to get cracking," clearly relishing all the phrase invoked of honest application, homespun values, a vanishing wilderness. "There are times," Loophole intoned, not so much to Al as to the fetor Gilhooley had left in her waddling wake, "when life catches up with you, when all that allowed you to proceed with your plans at your own pace can no longer be counted on. They're on to me," he groaned. "That's certain. They know They know that I sweep whatever they assign me out of the way as quickly as possible in order to get back to my excruciated incapacity to contemplate the emergence of my true work, my real work, my work of the future. They know." He was whispering shriekingly into Al's ear. "And suddenly you find yourself," he proceeded, "where you found yourself before all this paraphernalia permitting you to proceed with your own plans, etc., intervened on behalf of your destitution. And looking back you wonder how the little bit of security induced by the fates' wan smile caused you to stray so far from connectedness—connectedness as readiness, connectedness as crouched preparedness for the worst these fates might subsequently hurl down—to that initial destitution. Now that the paraphernalia is being swept away—for it is clear they won't keep me much longer, her little visit just now was a way of testing me, exasperating me, punishing me, seeing how much I can take—I wonder how I could have remained blind for so long to the premonitory signs of a catastrophe that has always been hanging over me. But I mustn't blame myself. Aren't there enough imbeciles out there to do that for me." Al did not feel in any way attacked by this last remark. He seemed gratified almost to the point of complacency by what he was undergoing as a remorseful outpouring. A whiff of this complacency induced in Loophole a more vehement venomous intensity of whispered shrieks. But as he shrieked he was hard put to locate the precise target of his indisputably venomous vehemence. The target was not quite Gilhooley, nor was it Al. "It is only now that these last years, these furiously tranquil years with Flatulong and his whole crew, begin to stink of a long sleep, a long lapse from self-preservation. What were they but a puff pastry stretched to bursting." "Maybe," said Al, "you're forgetting here tonight the very real confrontations, the very real agonies, that were undergone during the period in question." Al sounded as if he were speaking to him through a bullhorn, from a long way off. His sudden unctuous helpfulness, his lumpish brotherly tact, was devised to modulate the bullhornish resonance unavoidable when bellowing across a steep and sand-swept distance. Loophole shook off this suggestion more abruptly than he thought he had intended to. "Now it seems as if those confrontations and agonies were merely mock-confrontations, mock-agonies, devised to keep me insulated, cut off from the real confrontations which, had I met them head-on at the decisive moment, would have steered me far from where I presently find myself, reunited with a boglike plight from which I have never, in fact, been separated. Just as destitute as before I am in fact more destitute precisely because I have had no interim practice in being destitute. But soon I will be having lots of practice. Do you hear, lots of practice? Now that Gilhooley, pressured by her sultan, is pressuring me outside office hours, reminding me on my own time that I am not paid to sit on my fat ass, I begin to realize that this working life, this epoch of manly breadwinning activity—which I both took for granted as an insignificant and eminently expendable pastime (perversely pursued simply because I was intrigued by its very gratuitousness, its contextless and sequestered futility) and wore like a second skin, like a resuscitating prosthesis—is coming to a close. And so, as I said, there will be lots of practice. But how could I have allowed myself to be lulled for so long and to such a degree and by such a spurious calm." Loophole knew he would strangle Al if he attempted to answer. He watched the young couple who had been feeding on pastries emerge from the kitchen to shake hands variously with Flatulong and some of the other guests the majority of whom—if Flatulong's guffawingly complacent growl was to be believed—maintained their very own private planes for business and for pleasure. Exalted company, this. Gilhooley tried to edge her way into the group. She had delivered her message and now she was pretending to be beyond painfully striving to be something more, far more, than a mere underling.

He watched them chat, Gilhooley volunteering a few garbled rejoinders. He watched Al watching but Al's watching was watching of a completely different order—watching that was admiring and without rancor. No danger of conspecificity of watchings even if the watchers in question had once been chained, in amity, to the same cushion. With Al's purity of example before him Loophole wondered if his rage was not in fact deforming everything in sight, deforming a perfectly natural, certainly delightful, interchange among some highly placed and rightfully prominent business people into egregious and irrefutable proof of the world's vacuity. Even the most crystalline and apodictic discernment was invalidated by a driving force so easily isolated and defined. He was scorned, neglected, deemed unworthy on every front, and was therefore blackening all that unfolded before him. His grandiose effects were all attributable to the puniest of causes. The cause bracketed him away from all grandiosity. He sneered at himself. Convinced that he was looking down at all of being—for wasn't all of being assembled here tonight—from an unattainable height he was in fact already assimilated as a speck to some alien perspective. Whose? By what was he already absorbed? He looked hard at the little circle of victors, chatting, fondling each other's banalities, and it came to him. He was already absorbed by their total indifference not only to what he thought his gaze revealed of indecipherably lofty verdict but to what it actually divulged of disappointment, defeat, despair, dread, decay. He was not, as he wished to think, far outside their domain, outside their ken of classification. Rather he was very much, in his raw susceptibility of the last few hours, at the heart of their classification system, diagnosed and consigned for all eternity to some shanty in Siberia. But then as he went on watching, still differently from gaping Al, as he watched them rattle off the monumental insignificances of their daily life, finding common interests right and left, revelling in their shared disgust at bad highways, rude taxi drivers, disgruntled elevator boys, he wondered if rage had not in fact now depopulated of all blurring intimidatedness his perception of these puppets. Hadn't rage been a veritable passageway to discovery. Or was rage in fact simply deforming everything at the behest of its essential impotence. He tried to resolve the matter. But there was no resolving it. The truth of rage lay in the uncomfortable oscillation among these two irreconcilable possibilities. Turning to Al, Loophole saw that he had fallen into a kind of blissful stupor, of fascinated delight. But there was no time to try to edge in on the stupor, to bury himself in its folds, for here was Gilhooley once again bearing down on him with new instructions, presumably. Yet as she advanced she seemed to be making a concentrated effort not to see him, to look his way, to know him. She would know him only when it came time to give him his orders. "You have to start moving on these ideas," she said loudly, so that Flatulong could take it all in from his post at the hors-d'oeuvres table. She was hoping to impress him with her forceful masterful manipulation of underlings. "We've simply been putting out too much money. It isn't fair to Mr. Flatulong." She did not seem to notice the look of revulsion in her interlocutor and it was precisely this thickness of her skin that got under his own, the fat couched in fat enabling her to overcome any scruples. He looked at her with total expressionlessness, with all the stoic grimness of subcutaneous rage—for didn't these reprimands come down to nothing less than being taken away from his true work or rather from that contracted space, that space of a contraction, in which he was able to contemplate the failure of the true work to arrive consummated and fully decked out on

131

the doorstep of his assiduous anticipation—but she did not flinch, her eyeballs merely quivered away, not to the right or left but further back into their rheumy surface. He strained toward her lest he miss a word. But she was now mumbling as she was wont to do and seemed at the same time vexed at his inability to render lucid at a moment's notice this whimpering incoherence. She was clearly ashamed of her defective paraphrase of all Flatulong had told her to say without preamble. Her eyes blamed him for her own dullness, her inability to transform all this stammering into forthright directive. Unable to stop himself, he simply moved off and away, leaving her to contend with Al's homage-laden stupor as best she might. Lou was now sitting alone in a corner. He advanced on him. He needed someone to speak to, a target for ravenous oratory. He needed some slightly skeptical bulk to render plausible the self-defense that was rising up within him. He needed to make himself visible to her in his essence. Once she recognized him as the truest incarnation of . . . himself she, Gilhooley, would pardon this abrupt departure. Once she recognized that he could not be straitjacketed, bracketed away, that his rapturous fealty to the crystalline setting of the azure, for example, translated far from the vicinity of her underlings and rendered him unlocalizable, undiagnosable, forever mysterious—once she recognized all this through the swelling of his periods she would beg him to return to the fold. He would be able to depend on her respectful reliance on his views and opinions. In pursuance of this end, he intoned loudly, tremblingly, to Lou's right ankle, "I would love to run away . . . " He was moved to tears by his undulating evocation of flight to pastures new, to the safety of ramparts tinted gold by the waning rays of the sun, to . . . It seemed as if everyone was lulled—Gilhooley, Flatulong and all the others. Those who had been reaching for their hat and coat stopped dead in their tracks, delivered up to the unimpeachable purity of a nacreous blue, a coppery red. The more he delineated of this tender scene, the more those among whom it still surprised him to find himself prostrated themselves before its limitless expanse. Gilhooley and Flatulong had never looked so malleable. Was he drunk or were they bleary-eyed with the promise of just the sort of recognition he sought. Loophole went on and on, surveying the meadows and valleys and unanticipated tarns clotted with birch stumps with the same wonderment as his auditors. The more he delineated the more fabulous was the agglomeration of perfectly meshed detail. Yet the more he delineated the more plugged through and through with contingency, restriction. obstacle became his creation. Awareness of this was inseparable from the awareness that his enunciated dream was drawing to a close. At its conclusion, as if speaking for everyone, Lou said, "It's not hard to sympathize with the desire to escape." It took only a second for these words to seep in. So this was what it came to in the end, all this rapturous exertion. Once more he was classified, caught in the web spun by his own daydream. He looked around. There was nothing to hope for from this crew, Gilhooley was lost to him forever.

He had hoped that at least one of them would have discerned the gap between what he was, what he was forced to undergo day after day, and what he was capable of synthesizing on the spur of the moment. He had expected to be in some way reverenced for his obvious abstention from all he had painted of pleasure, pastoral rapture, rapturous leisure. He had expected they would bow down in homage before his oscillation in the spaces between what he was, what he condemned himself to be, and what he was capable of delineating as an alternative, as an . . escape. How he loathed the word. Couldn't Lou see that he was superior to this stance of escape, that in depicting escape and its endpoint with so much audacious coloring and textural filigree he had in fact recoiled from both in time—or so he had believed—to reap, for this mammoth abstention in the name of drudgery unsung, his rightful reward of a reverence that would, alas, never now be his

Delineating what he had delineated he believed himself outside all stances, neither within his drudgery as a satellite of Flatulong nor condemned to waste away within the confines of a topography a little too opulent in valleys, grottoes, streams and pastures. But here he was, all too intelligible, refuted in his dimensionless oscillation to the straitjacket of a single stance. He was Loophole, the one who longed to escape, the one who longed from his position of abject fixity. They felt toward him, these amiable listeners who had come along for the ride, as he had felt toward his brother-in-law enacting his own turbulence. Only now it was he who was far far too conspicuous for his own good. Gilhooley was a little turned away from him. The more he had delineated the more he had believed, needed to believe, he would be enshrined among them as the one who, though capable of inventing and therefore possessing the beautiful, did not succumb to the lure. How foolish he had been. "What an imbecile," he muttered to himself. For these he was very much more a specimen than a hero. They could only take a voluptuous pleasure in condemning him as he who had given way before they did, who spared them the necessity of a similar descent into appalling . . . conspicuousness. He looked around. All these faces refuted him. Gilhooley, bloodthirstiest of the lot, refuted him. He was refuted not so much in his daydream as in this sense of himself as outside both the daydream and the dung of daily life in which the daydream, leafless, blossomless, had sprouted. For those assembled here he was very much inside the daydream, very much connected to the daydream in its damning because diagnosable particularity. Couldn't they see that all he had meant was that if ever he longed to escape he might fashion this particular topography, this particular confection. But it was very possible that he might fashion something altogether different. He was not to be bound to any particular confection. Every confection elaborated was to be thought of as the lowliest, or rather, the most accessible placeholder for what might be synthesized in the very distant future. But they were all binding him to this particular confection as the purest expression of his craving to be gone. to be far from where manly duty required that he be. He was intelligible, therefore disfigured. He could feel his limbs crumbling.

They all looked as if his whole past history of wartlike defects coming, like savings bonds, to tumultuous and wartlike maturity, could be deduced from the daydream. There was nothing left to lose. He was an open and shut case. His days, his minutes, with the firm were numbered. He looked around for Lou. Only Lou could get him out of this labyrinth. But Lou was nowhere to be found. So he did the next best thing, he took Al, casting commiserating glances at Gilhooley, to one side and said, "This obsession with work is a waste of time, Al." This was the first time, to his knowledge, he called him Al. Al bristled slightly at being so pelleted."Until one finds a spot, Al, one is pantingly eager to be placed. One literally slobbers after the conferring of this supreme sign of worthiness. One does not like to be out in the cold, idle. But once obtained, the job as a test of one's intrinsic worth quickly disintegrates and one is left with a lump, a mottled foul-smelling residue of obligations. This residue is the work at hand, performed for the benefit and enrichment of those one can only detest. And every time one feels the least bit of enthusiasm—" here his voice grew louder and louder so that Gilhooley had literally to cover her ears though her better half did not seem in the least intimidated by the clamor —"enthusiasm for this work at hand—excruciation increases exponentially with the realization that one's being is being flexed and extended in the shadowy domain of the bloodsucking enemy. Once obtained, the job proves to be the measure of nothing but one's capacity to keep raging revulsion within bounds." "But doesn't that count for something?" Al asked. There was a certain effaced shrewdness in his tone that intrigued Loophole, almost put him to sleep. "Hell man," Al went on, but more blusteringly as if ashamed of whatever latent tenderness Loophole had detected in his previous

tone, "you work to put the bacon on the table. Simple as that.'
Loophole smiled. He could feel himself smiling. This was a new
sensation. He tried to make the smile mournful, ironical, but it
was too late. He was already irradiated with enthusiasm. He no
longer had to rage against Gilhooley. He was obliged to work. His
descent daily into his cubicle was not a perverse whim, relentlessly
resurrected. There was no longer a need to act on his rage. There
was no longer a need to provoke her to fire him because he was
too cowardly to leave on his own steam. He had to stay. Keeping
his loathing, his disgust, in bounds was no longer the pusilan-
imous dissimulation of what a real man would have brought into
the open long before. Keeping his disgust within bounds was a
symptom of . . . slowly thickening ripeness.
He looked around for Gilhooley. He wanted to welcome himself
back into her fold. She was nowhere in sight. Where was
she—why was she tormenting him again albeit, now, with her
inaccessibility. Before he could dismiss his misgivings as mere
chimeras, they were once again engorged with their old virulence.
He loathed her. How he loathed her. He loathed her passionately,
as the sign and summary of every possible humiliation to which
his kind was susceptible once embarked on its chosen course. He
loathed her for not being here, to witness and beatify his
transformation. There was a tap on his shoulder. At last. She, it
had to be she. He was ready to forgive her her waddle, her
whine, her refusal to be moved by his recent flight of fancy.
Turning he saw Lou whose resemblance to the now absent Al
was nothing less than startling. "Your trouble with her," Lou
said, "stems from your never having accepted once and for all
your loathing, your rage, your disgust. Right. You're not alone.
I can't stand her either." Loophole thought he would faint for
here she was, as usual when most unwanted, bearing down upon
them, newly afflicted with an uncontrollable contortedness
inhabiting her stride and disclosing an awareness that her name
had been uttered but not in a friendly way. "But I accept my

loathing and her loathsomeness and go on from there," Lou continued, with Gilhooley standing no more than two feet away and clearly intent on catching every word. "But you," he proclaimed, jabbing Loophole's sternum with his pudgy thumb, "you wallow in and exaggerate your loathing precisely because you have not yet begun to believe, cannot bear to believe, in her intrinsic loathsomeness. You exaggerate your loathing in order to somehow displace attention from the loathsomeness of its target to the legitimacy, now dubious, of the loathing itself. Loophole, you rant and rave to make yourself conspicuous to your target, to induce some kind of dressing down, some kind of gesture that will rob you of your need to rant and rave any longer. You go on believing her, despite all evidence to the contrary, a friend, a friendly force, able to afford you the recognition you hopelessly crave. At this rate you will never begin the true work, as either work for them or for yourself alone. How can you begin if you have yet to make sure once and for all that she is favorably disposed toward your efforts, that she is, for all her bustling opposedness, in fact deep inside the throes of amity, of good intentions." "And you," said Loophole, limply, ashamed to be soliciting wise counsel from this hulk, "what's your approach." "Whereas I, Loophole," Lou continued blithely as if he had not been interrupted by this diffident plea, "whereas I, have long ago set her to the side as a force of pure destructiveness, pure negativity, within whose radius I must nevertheless continue to work, strive to work, strive to work to earn my daily bread and feed the missus and the little ones. Put her to the side, Loophole, or you'll never get started. Set her aside, bracket her, even if you know you've been set down in the very midst of her capacity to thwart your every move." Lou terminated his peroration with a little sigh as Gilhooley hurried off limping. Loophole watched her every move toward the toilet, presumably in search of Flatulong. But he was too busy eating and invoking all the friends who maintained their very own private planes to notice this hobbling abjection with rage at its heart. With one hand on a fleshily indignant hip and the other on the doorknob, she stationed herself between the sink and the tub, stamping her foot with nervous insistence, as if to remain always slightly ahead of the rhythm of some popular tune. Her eyes, visibly bloodshot, even at that distance, with slovenly reproach, were drawn to the site of almost intolerable humiliation. She had clearly heard enough to need to blame someone for all the echo of her eavesdropping was continuing to provoke of burning discomfort, of authentic turmoil. He turned from her bloody gaze, dreading to consider what his status must now be. Would she fire him as soon as she finished stamping her foot. As there was no telling how soon the blow would come, he closed his eyes, here, in the middle of a crowded room. The atoll greenery was refunded but only for the briefest of intervals. Opening his eyes he thought immediately of his wife and child. Before the knot their hapless image induced in his bowels could grow any more involuted he turned back to Gilhooley. Ruminating on their inevitable destitution he could only wonder, Was it too late to make amends, was it too late to bracket her loathsomeness and his loathing and get back to work. She was no longer toilet-bound, he saw. Her being nowhere in sight he took, absurdly, for a sign of enhanced susceptibility to some form of plea, some form of ragged importunity on behalf of the loved ones. I'll be good from now on, he wanted to cry, I'll be good. He wanted to inform her he was at last miraculously disembarrassed of debilitating torment at the ever recurring sight of the signposts of his true—his truest—work completely submerged beneath the sludge of a life that did not appertain in the least to his destiny. Yet she must be made to understand, now that his loathing was once and for all bracketed, that he didn't mind being coupled to a life that appertained not in the least to his destiny—nor to a job that appertained not in the least—nor to an employer that, etc. As long as he was allowed to continue bringing home the bacon. She must be made to understand he had given up for good the need to sustain the illusion of a daily grind, in this case ground out behind the partition of his very own windowless cubicle, somehow partaking of a true work's quintessence. He was ready to accept his life as a waste, an irrelevance, a permanent estrangement from what might have been, needed to be, if he was to have had any hope of looking back blissful on authentic achievement. Accepting all this, he could only look upon the bracketing—straitjacketing—of rage as child's play. Just as he was beginning to think, with a shudder, that they had every intention of getting rid of him he collided with her. She smiled, popping a puff pastry of especially delicate consistency into Flatulong's mouth. Long before the complaisant fingertips were out of the vicinity of the prehensile and voracious palate Loophole found himself well on his way to Lou, or was it Al, in quest of a more pondered perspective on this little tableau and what it could possibly bode for his future. Lou laughed when he noted the worry constricting Loophole's features. "No, no, no," he belched. "They have absolutely no intention of getting rid of you. So what if you curse them, so what if you oppose to their little tasks the sabotaging immensity of the projected true work. Their capacity to exploit is inconceivably vaster than all your efforts at frantic computation founded, much too punily, on the titration of what you produce for them against that which you smuggle away on your own behalf might lead you to believe. Merely assured of your showing up, your presence, your skinny ass hugging the revolving stool, they go on to net a profit whose dimensions—rather, whose dimensionlessness—your tools could never hope to mar. Not with all the sabotaging dedication in the world. You're done for, man. That is to say, you'll never be fired. They need you—as a placeholder." These were the words he longed to hear, they assured him he and his beloveds would survive but now that survival was assured he was overcome by a million and one needs infinitely more potent than survival and in relation to which the certainty of survival was at best an obstruction. He had no choice but to flee, into the street and uptown along the East River flowing. The movement of the belt of cars, taxicabs and trucks along the highway was less authentic movement than an alluvial deposit, ornamented with luminous pinpricks, of the day's defunct and frenzied surrender to movement —less movement than a kind of after-thought, refluxed commentary slowed down to super-legibility, on the madness of movement. From the distance a figure tried to catch up with his meditations. Loophole looked up: the moon, cloud like gibbous, had just been netted by the sprawling foliage of a penthouse rooftop. Still distant the figure called, with a mixture of imperiousness and senile querulousness that made him first hesitate then hasten his steps. Loophole, hey Loophole. In a minute he knew it was Lou, or Al, coming to straitjacket him anew, deliver him up to the more buxom diagnosing competence of the higher-ups. Before he could surrender to expatiation on the beauty of the belt, of the moon appended to stratospheric spray—before he could, with awesome rapture, overwhelm this advancing other beyond its crouched craving to label, label, label—before the rapture could refute any verdict on rapture hoping to skulk away smirking and unscathed—the other, it turned out to be Al, said, "You were right." "How so," Loophole challenged. The sky, darkly descending the way he had come, was chiselled all down the serrated edge of monumental oblongs."They told me to tell you you can stay. Your past has caught up with you. But even after seeing that you are completely unfit for all other species of toil they are not sending you away. They want you back. They told me to tell you you can stay—"Loophole coughed to show his impatient indifference to their liberality. "Your past has caught up with you but they don't intend to stand by and gloating snicker over your newly revealed inherent destitution. Your past has caught up with you but—" "But it isn't my past," Loophole finally exploded. "It's as much mine as your shadow converging on my meditations a few minutes back. Yes, yes, yes, the past has caught up with me but it isn't my past, it is no sum

140

of evasions to which my own—very own—pusillanimity can lay claim. Somebody else's past riddled with the usual egregious errors and miscalculations has been visited upon me, grafted onto my losing battle with the powers that be. Yet I understand all these alien but perfectly typical miscalculations. It might as well be my past. In short, I formally adopt it as my own. In short, I'm myself no longer. I accept the consequences of another's mistakes as that other—or some other—must end up accepting the consequences of mine. In short, I'll be in on Monday. Happy New Year. I'll be on time. Not the least bit hung over." Loophole noticed that Al was growing uncomfortable. "I have to be getting back to the party," he said. "To Flatulong and company," Loophole countered brutally. "They wanted to make sure there were no . . . hard feelings. No hard feelings on the job." Remembering that he had renounced all claim to the true work—at least for now—for as long as he was spared provocation by Gilhooley, by Flatulong, by their haphazardly concocted assignments—remembering, he managed to synthesize a smile almost rancid in its sweetness which proclaimed: No hard feelings.

Picked up on the Highroad (Out)

I was picked up on the high road out. The fading flowers were almost orotund in the obligatory glow of sky before dark and damp. Many thoughts assailed but more important was the following: Were those assailing those I had been looking for all along or were they merely the most accessible substitute for what I insisted on evading. I could not determine the sex of the pilgrims up ahead, chanting like birds before the storm, because the rumps were draped in heavy sackcloth. Whispers. One stared straight ahead, recovering from foray on a coveted lobe. He could have been speaking of the landscape and here he was facing it anew. Having transformed it he was awaiting and defying a reprisal. Another approached but instead of going straight up to the others sat himself down on a rock and proceeded to draw on the right kneecap with the nail of the left forefinger. Chortling, the others pointed, these were not ones to miss out on an opportunity for deriding the tics of a comrade. Guffawing they clung to their paunches as if saddlebags mercilessly shaken by the impetuosity of hot steeds encountering the smoky tortuosities of the route. The new arrival began to interest me, exiled from his congeners he at once became sole signpost in a mounting, always mounting, maze of detours and dead ends. As he nodded to what he had just drawn I could not decide whether the nod belonged to the tic or served as its fire exit. Was this nod not in fact a commentary, sombre yet not without pity, on those who, too precipitously, had insisted on coupling him irreversibly to the unfolding of the tic. One looked with especial ill intent.

143

Another's derisive laughter served as goad to this first who then tried through the variegation of his gasps and groans to surpass somehow the laughter's even tempered mutuality. The second was content to be even tempered: But then the first, whom it's best to call Neddie, began to wonder if the second, whom we have no choice but to call Eddie, was laughing not at the kneecap across the way but at him, Neddie. At this point it looked as if Neddie's bilious fear was provoking a frantic inventory of every word and gesture paid out from sunset on. But how can I be sure and being sure arrange for others to undergo what I found myself undergoing as I witnessed that frantic inventory. Eddie looked at the third figure but without Neddie's insane virulence. Sinking into his looking he seemed forever on the verge of comment. But though the gaze remained firmly fixed on its target it always swerved away just in the nick of time. Neddie too looked on the verge of words but words did not come. Not because he was unequal to the uttering but rather because in advance he knew it could never be strong enough to undo, do away with, the third. But how do I know this. I watched Neddie. He looked as if he was acting out on the words he failed to speak whatever rage and contempt he refused to lavish on the etched patella. Let us call Freddie the proprietor of the etched patella. Freddie Watson, Freddie Hopkins, Freddie Watson-Hopkins. Freddie Watkins, there, it's settled. More pilgrims began to appear and Freddie trailed after them, straining beyond the rise and fall of his thighs. I tried to catch a glimpse of the drawing but if it did exist it was hidden by foliage and by an appended shrub of ridicule, pith of the exchanges between Eddie and Neddie. Freddie could not keep up with the contemplated target of presently obstructed contemplation and so ended up speaking to the pile of knapsacks the other pilgrims left behind. This I know, this I saw. But just because I know and saw this does not mean others will be able to know and see as I have known, seen.

The moon rendered the knapsacks incandescent. Freddie took the flicker of light over the wrinkled leather for a kind of innuendo. How do I know this. It sounded as if he was explaining his future duties to them, the duties that would overtake him when the highroad came to an end at the threshold of the halfway house. The knapsacks did not look as if they required information but speaking of his duties Freddie found them less terrifying. He attributed all of his ambivalences toward those duties to the knapsacks piled high in the moonlight. Yet how do I know this. Looking around, Freddie found himself alone and in the un-enviable position of one saddled with a targetless vigilance. Neddie had risen and moved away, calling back, "I'll be back soon," the wavering in his bravado-laden baritone knew that he would not soon be missed. But ever-widening distance from the point of origin—the stump on which he and Eddie had been deriding their congener—attenuated his absurdity and invested him with a little grandeur even. He was dwarfed and thereby aggrandized by his own motions. He was no longer Neddie but a high-stepping demiurge plowing through shrubs and parting their thighs without the least trepidation. The pilgrims returned, among them Eddie and Neddie. One pilgrim approached him. "Where's the guy supposed to be guarding our knapsacks?"that one asked Eddie. "The rest room," Eddie replied. That reply transformed him into Freddie's caretaker though it was possible that his derision had, from the start, been paternalistically well-intentioned. A father wants his son to rise in the world and he will not stop short of—nay will actively exploit—intimidating ridicule to stimulate the brash persistence the planet requires of its tyros. Eddie repeated, "The rest room." In the repetition his inflection was a little different, it was clear it was no pleasure to live inside the implications of his paternity, but it might have made any man peevish to be progenitor of such an implausible prodigy. As he spoke Eddie looked not at me, not at his interlocutor, not at the spot previously occupied by the Freddie

145

orating before the knapsacks, but at some distant, perhaps imaginary, point on the horizon. Remembering Freddie among the knapsacks frightened Eddie. How do I know. Remembering Freddie among the knapsacks seemed to frighten Eddie. And as he went on uttering, giving in the end far more than had been required by the impatient pilgrim standing before him, the words became less a means of telling all about Freddie than a blanket haphazardly sewn on which to lay out for cautious, all too cautious, inspection the terminally luminous dregs of a mammoth fear. But why should Freddie frighten Eddie, frighten anybody. Freddie returned a little after the pilgrim departed. It was not clear whether or not he had adequately wiped the cleft in his hindquarters. He had the look of one who wipes inadquately and who yearns with and from his whole being for the rigorous parental upstroke, lost forever. Freddie sat down. Let me call him more than Freddie, let me call him Freddie Watkins, no more than Freddie Watkins, Freddie Watkins Dune-Buggy, so that he does not, as a result of my negligence in naming often enough or for some other reason, disintegrate. For he already looked half washed away by this inadmissible craving for a strong hand sheathed in its gritty dishrag. Seeing Eddie, Freddie got up to go to him, Eddie tried to look absorbed by the point on the horizon soon to be named after him. But, alas, Eddie was not all that convincing as a looker, he was always too much forever on the brink of looking. He was either too appalled or too little affected by his professed target to achieve or achieving persist in immersion. In short, he kept an eye out on Freddie slowly advancing. "Freddie," he murmured, and then he turned to, turned on, the one to whom the murmured name referred, either to celebrate his own thralldom to the unearthly resonance of the name once murmured or to tantalize himself deridingly with all the little gestures, Freddie-spawned, that failed to find, or prove themselves worthy of, shelter within, deep inside, the folds of the name. Or perhaps he turned to Freddie to prove to himself that he continued to exist and had by no means been definitively obliterated through the naming. Or perhaps it saddened and comforted him, both, to see Freddie decked out in his little gestures striving in vain beyond the confines of the name which striving only ended up affirming the power of the name. So much for Eddie, who looked for himself and for his absent crony. A heavy rain began to fall. How do I know. No, how can I let others know. No, how can others be made to undergo what, undergone only by me, by me alone, threatens to unseam my precarious equilibrium. The drops began to obliterate the sheen on the knapsacks. At the first sound of the drops on the shrubs' flattened leaves Freddie leaped into the heap. There. Others can, on the basis of these proffered details, undergo what I have undergone. Or rather, while they are busy struggling to metabolize these details they can be thought of as, willy-nilly, effecting the transformation of the landscape into the scene of downpour. Neddie returned with the end of the rain. It is tempting to call Neddie an anachronism in any epoch. He was in his own way fastidious though at times he had limited or no control over his viscera which ended up colliding as if on skates. But he was hoping, how do I know, hoping like the rest of us whether we wanted to admit it or not, that the halfway house would resolve all difficulties. Before he had a glimmer of who he was he knew he had to be rehabilitated. Eventually all was still, my cohorts, for now they were my cohorts though they gleamed not in purple and gold, surrendered to sleep and sleeping the sleep of the dead gurgled blissfully. I could not sleep. I waited. The others snored. I became aware of the passing of time. Time did not stand still for the pilgrim who had questioned Eddie was huddled up to one side and no longer nurturing exasperation. I would have liked that pilgrim to remain exasperated forever. Incapable of showing interest in the sleepers I did the next best thing, I interrogated the landscape, I made friends with the broad boles for boles are a helpmate especially when knobbed and burled and streaked with the shadow of their overhanging ramifications. I began to confuse them with my ancestors. I began to desire them. Yes, desire them. Desiring them I felt myself becoming limitless, big as all of being. It was only when I began to think of desire as a symptom that I smelled a configuration around the bend, felt myself turning into something loathsome — something bounded, frontiered, like Eddie, Neddie, Freddie, and their ilk. But I consoled myself saying that if anyone at the halfway house dared to label me, name me, as Eddie had named Freddie, saddle me with an infirmity, I would wiggle out, quickly defect to another, and become neither one nor the other but the shuttle between, incessant and blithely blasphemous. With dawn the boles receded. But desire did not. In the first gusts of the new day each tree became a house divided — twig against twig, branch against branch. It was as if I was at the bottom of the sea, among jousting crustaceans.

There was nothing in the configuration of the new dawn that seemed to offer an apology for its essential sameness. Always the same thrusts from under the same sloped shoulder whose stench was, under no circumstances, to be parried. Just before the boles were completely out of sight desire attained its zenith. Yet what was desire made of but a doomed craving to puncture the boles' bubble of obliviousness to that desire. And what could I have done with the boles suddenly deigning to have some sort of truck with desire, my desire, what more than abscond in shame with the booty of their fleetingly fraternizing glance directed a little to the right or left of my center of gravity. I pretended for the benefit of those awakening or for the benefit of myself soon to be confronted with the ill intentions of those awakening that I was doing research on boles. So what if instead through them research was in fact being done on me. I did not have time to wonder what monster pen in claw was charting my progress through fructive bogs. I kept away from the other pilgrims, from the timbre of their spluttering outcries I deduced the various stages of their ablutions. When they moved I too, cautiously, moved. I interpreted that movement on the soft earth as their go-ahead signal, as a go-ahead signal from the universe itself, but to do what, what exactly. Or I could have moved to camouflage the deafening roar of my listening to their every movement or to distract myself from the excruciation inseparable from a waiting for their attack or worse their solicitude. But how can I say why I moved. I moved. The speculation comes later, not to explain, not to clarify, but to suture the wound born of moving. Each exegetical moment is a stitch. I was not born to move. I was born to stand still, to abstain, and to await compensation for my abstention. I tried to wander off, to look like I was leaving them for good, like pollen perishing on the daylight breeze. But before I could vanish—or rather, before I could profit from my own absence—I felt myself becoming an object, more than an object, a flagrant and fatuous image of lumpish desolation, stodgy stasis. Faster than I could escape I became a directionless sign of escape, the absolute value of escape. Whatever of doomed futile stumbling was pointed to, at, by the word, escape, I embodied lavishly. So I had no choice but to return, to Eddie, Neddie, Freddie, and company. None would speak to me, not even Freddie, who seemed comfortable shackled to his fleering congeners, who seemed to be thriving beneath the wheels of the mobile inquisitory destined for the halfway house. Maybe he fancied himself a consul reposing on his sedan chair. I should have known better than to expect a scapegoat to be grateful for my charity. Yet what had this legendary charity consisted of anyway. He looked on me, this was clear, even though he never turned my way, as a mere impediment on the way back to the warming stench emitted by his tormentors. Freddie clearly wanted to be rehabilitated and he was taking the babble of Eddie and Neddie for a kind of expert preliminary diagnosis. How do I know. I tried to overtake him, I tried to warn him, he was not yet inside the halfway house, there was no reason why he had to yield himself so prematurely as inquisitory fodder. He had a right to enjoy his last moments before the emblazoned gates closed permanently on his harlequinade. At my cry he turned back as he continued to move. Eddie and Neddie did likewise, watching them I began to understand walking for the first time, I began to see what walking means. I understood walking at the moment when another action challenged and competed with and threatened to uproot it, went against its grain. Freddie stopped for he had nothing of his masterly comrades' adeptness at doing two things at once. Beware of the stench, I cried. He asked me what stench I was talking about. The question wounded me. I needed a seam for this newborn fissure. I needed a thought, thoughts, to combat this thought, lowly Freddie's thought, Freddie's lowly thought, assaulting from without. I exploded with something like, The wind is in the tree. There, that's better. But that thought too, my very own no less, wounded and as deeply, even more deeply, and once uttered the lesion of its echo craved no suture. Still another suturing thought became necessary, therefore, and doublequick. Although I could feel myself overflowing with thoughts like, A stitch in time saves the halfway house, and, Inquisitors are bloodier than their own blood, and, There stands the remnants of my being, I knew deep down that the best thoughts were found coilingly clustered about events that could be tortured and twisted into an ambiguity requiring, for successful smothering and obliteration, a trickle of explanations. So I purposefully strained toward those states of affairs inside the landscape with the proper look of ambiguous leaning. But the more I strained the more the landscape refused to decompose into discrete states of affairs, much less discretely ambiguous ones. So there was no saddling myself with suturing explaining thoughts born from a contrived perplexity in the face of phenomena.

I began to feel that my straining, my tenacity in straining toward absolutely nothing in sight, was the only in any way ambiguous state of affairs. I was hungry to explain, to think my explanations, but everything out there was dead and buried. I gave up on explanations and thinking said, I undergo strenuous incubation in this bloated half-dusk. The thought resonated a wee bit. I lived in the resonance. After the resonance was over I would know whether or not it was a suturing resonance but for the time being I was brought to a full stop and installed far from the groping clawing hunger for explaining thoughts. For the moment I was oscillating at a frequency insusceptible to the hunger for explanations. I forgot Freddie and Eddie and Neddie. This thought succeeded in cutting me off from them, from the anguish their proximity induced regarding all that must await me within the precincts of the halfway house. I was in fact cut off from the world, from all of being, I no longer succumbed to the connection. Living, nay celebrating, the utter irrelevance of my thought, my newfound minion, to anything familiar, to anything plausibly out there or within, I must have appeared strange to Eddie, Neddie and Freddie. But very quickly I found myself divining the meaning of my thought. Very quickly, it was showing itself reluctant to soothe me with its proud inapplicability to the things, the orts, of the world. Very quickly it was tracing itself in me as a kind of prophecy. Dusk was suddenly falling and it was turning out bloated and I was turning out to be strenuously incubating, but what was I incubating, what in fact was I incubating. I wanted to weep, end it all.

This thought, in proclaiming and affirming—worse, inducing its own—connection with the things of the world—was indisputably just like all the other thoughts capable of wounding but not of suturing, capable only of crying out for further suture. I felt my little world—my little world on the way to the halfway house—collapsing. I wanted to say, My world is collapsing. But I was afraid, mortally afraid, of uttering such a diagnosis. I was afraid that diagnosing would only perpetuate my condition. Despite my fear I uttered, My world is collapsing. I thought Eddie and

Neddie would be forced to take note of my daring. They did not but I did reap an unexpected dividend from another quarter—uttering my diagnosis did not perpetuate but rather inaugurated the disintegration of all that came under the heading, redolent of maelstroms, my condition. Utterance turned out, at least in this case, to be the signal for collapse of all that was subtended in the angle of utterance. I felt stronger suddenly. Suddenly I could face the trio and those beyond. I felt suddenly so strong that . . . that . . . that . . . that . . . five falcons swooped toward the sooty pate of one of the grossest of the group. How do I know. How can I make others know, or rather undergo what I know. I no longer care. In fact I don't know if in fact five falcons did swoop toward the sooty pate. Are there falcons hereabouts. All I know now is that saying, Five falcons swooped, etc., I was annotating and invoking, both; slavishly reporting and insolently fabricating, both. I was either annotating or invoking, neither annotating or invoking. I don't know what I was doing and my uncertainty, the tension and relief born of the tension's crystallization, in uncertainty, rescues me from the need to make others undergo what I know through having never undergone. Take me or leave me, that is what I wanted to say, this is what my gaze did say, to the pilgrims. For the first time I was at ease enough to notice Eddie's bleached sideburns and the frantic agglomeration of curls along the nape of the gracelessly balding Neddie. I made haste to tap Freddie on the shoulder. I felt as if I was tapping his latent resources, showing him the way to their optimal exploitation. Tapping, I pointed not to Eddie nor to Neddie but rather to the space between my two monumental discoveries. When he did not seem to be catching on I drew my forefinger along the back of my neck and then puttered with that same forefinger between ear lobe and jawbone. Still not catching on he forced me to murmur, "Matinee idols." The thought, uttered, became as strange to me as the phenomenon out there it was supposed to have tamed and dragged intact to its lair. I fought with the echoing echo of the words of the thought until it became clear that these words, this worded thought, was less about the sideburns and the frantic compensatory proliferation of sooty tendrils than about its own failure to exorcise the demon with which it had been recruited to do combat. Using these words, riding pillion on the wings of this worded thought, I had tried to enlist Freddie, in what, against what. Freddie turned away. Either he did not understand or did not want to understand or act on what he understood. He went back to Neddie and Eddie. Only Isador seemed to look like he might welcome my company. I sat down beside him at the campfire. He ate his beans and tapped his cowboy boots with his spoon.

I tried to look respectful of Isador's right to be a cowboy, to strive to be a cowboy. He was after all convinced that he was indeed a cowboy. Cowboy while you can, I wanted to say in a kindly way. But not knowing how my inflection would turn out I said nothing. Staring into the fire I felt so situated as to be able to achieve a rehabilitation—minute, momentous, instantaneous— at the hands of one who had clearly surpassed all his symptoms. Though why he was on his way, or our way, to the halfway house remained a mystery still. I could not bear to believe that one who was able to wear his sombrero at an angle of such self-satisfied—self-satisfied though by no means smug—rakishness might at the same time be malformed and in need of help. "Well," he suddenly said mounting above a belch, "let's bring all these warring feelings to the surface, man." "I always do . . . bring them to the surface." Without looking I knew his hatted head was sadly shaking. He said what I brought to the surface, high above the surface in fact, were slogans, labels, not feelings. And these slogans nipped in the bud and annihilated whatever it was they professed to circumscribe and define. Every one of these slogans, labels, catchall diagnoses, then became an icon, a lodestone, to which I subsequently returned, over and over, for sheltering foothold. "So what," I sneered. "In that way I usurp the prerogative of my detractors." "None more merciless than yourself," he quipped, chewing a bean. I rose. I tried to depopulate that movement of all busy blustering indignation. I told him I had to watch the sun set. "You can watch it from here," he said, pointing to a near breach in the foliage. "But there is a particular vantage—" I began, but the words died, futile, on my breath. "The search for a vantage is the evasion of the vantage already accessible," he intoned but without rancor. Helping him out though why especially at that moment should I have wanted to help him out I added, "Quest for ostensibly more invigorating draughts is nothing but neglect of nearby nectar at the very least sufficiently potent for or against present purposes." I was competitively assisting in diagnosing the third party I had become. "You look for vantages because you are afraid of standing still," he concluded. Rising, Isadore eventually stood ten feet tall. But I immediately became tired of him, of his voice, or rather of his virtuosic shift among several voices all supple with importunity, scrupulously hesitant and deftly purged of any inflection that might, construed as incriminating, topple his tread on the tightrope of therapeutic tact. Suddenly I cried, "I know the best vantage from which to regard the sunset." I shrieked, gave way to falsetto. "I have proof," I added. He wasn't interested in my proof, though he did not, he told me, for a moment doubt that my proof was more than adequate. He was interested less in what I said than what it might be giving rise to within. By dawn I had still not made up my mind whether Izzy was friend or foe. I heard Eddie, Neddie and Freddie talking. They were now allies, indissolubly bound against. I heard them speaking of their future, bypassing the halfway house completely as if it was to be a mere interim, a brief stopover. Were they privy to some augur to which parrying Isador's blows had blinded me. I tried to tell myself that it is only when a pilgrim is most inextricably bound to the halfway house's protocol that he busily rehearses his imminent farewell. Profoundly encoiled he undergoes a slavish dependency as nothing less than the infinite freedom, infinite possibility of which his inquisitors are wishfully the supreme embodiment. Inseparable from, noisomely suffused with the sap of, thralldom he attains no vantage whence to intervene against the confusion of *fusion with* with *mastery of.* We began moving, vulnerability to every fork in the road was swallowed up in relief at the prospect of a terminus. I could never have propelled myself forward even among so many whose momentum was sure to keep sweeping me up and away if I had not been sure an endpoint, the halfway house, waited in ambush just as thinking out loud was impossible without a ready supply of platitudes. Isador appearing at my side appeared instinctively to understand that he was not to speak further of what had of late erupted before the campfire. If I had spoken to him of my plight, my infirmity, it would have been for the sole purpose of marking off that plight, that infirmity, against further reference. Wishing in spite of myself to speak I could only say, "The gut leaks." It was by no means the definitive articulation of whatever I was feeling but at least very quickly squelched any further need to make myself known to myself. "The gut leaks" did not so much delimit and describe a prior feeling as induce from the particular configuration of its elements a new feeling. And so for a privileged interim I was neither the old nor the new but a tour guide as it were in the little tundra of both. We both felt the breeze. I wondered if the breeze was fraught with injunction or if it was the motion of the highest twigs that seemed to usher in an epoch big with injunction. Isador was not perplexed by such problems. How do I know. But this is not to say he was not moved and deeply by all that assaulted us of raw dapple and exotic zigzag. He was the more truly moved because he was not obliged to invest what he saw with what he refused to know he felt. Ostensibly most moved I was merely most irritated, the way a paramecium is irritated by every bloody morsel in its path. Long before the halfway house I noted that I did not love things more than Isador, or Eddie or Neddie or the now defunct Freddie, born to fall by the wayside. I was only always in infinitely greater need of a repository for the anguish all things engendered. Beginning to know this need in its nudity I found myself at the same time beginning to miss Isador. I wept as if he had already bid me adieu.

Siege

The siege always finds me in my greater glory, caparisoned in the style of those bygone days when men were always a little less than men yet pantingly eager nonetheless to explore some inner quirk risen to the pitch of obsession. The quirk exacts a payment in the form of campaigns. And because campaigners give up soon enough I come to believe in myself more and more as one who must succeed. Not so much, perhaps, from any intrinsic merit or fortitude even as from glaring comparison to all those so obligingly fallen to the wayside, waylaid out.

My first act was to rename the campaign. Once the campaign was renamed I was able to consecrate myself to its consummation. I hid myself in a woodland and sought out likely targets. The enslavement, however, of those I first espied would hardly have redounded to my credit, much less my honor. In awaiting the real quarry I fed myself on whatever I could drag away to my lair unnoticed. Scavenging I assured myself that I contributed notably to the balance of nature and all the time, even with my fingers greasy all down their lengths, swore that I was on the lookout and in no danger of missing a trick.

Eagerly I pounced. I invited this athletic young man, travelling alone, to my table. He ate ravenously, almost dropping his lenses into a soup concocted of the saps distilled from twigs and slugs. After he left it became painfully clear that I would have difficulty procuring once again so fully formed an adversary. Few could be expected to situate, shape and stage a comparably effortless and pondered opposition to whatever discernment managed to unearth and sequester of a sum of traits. I am unable to free myself of his memory. Cremated by the worms, still I go on hoping dispersion to the four winds will be stayed by his reconstitution of my hangdog look.

A Plight

I knew he was my man from a certain bearing espied from a distance, followed him in. Under other circumstances I might have taken hours deciding whether or not to enter, he enabled me to cut short the preliminaries. Usually I had to seduce the site but entering he looked as if he had already taken care of the dirty business with the dividend accruing to me. At that moment of entering we differed by less, far less, than any preassignable difference, in he went, I say, and I followed. In his presence or rather in anticipation of his presence (X. or rather, Y) I had the distinct, as opposed to the indistinct, impression that my most shameful traits were no less than finely-honed implements allowing for ironical self-repudiation as the language of truth. I sat down behind what I thought must be he. I knew it was he because 1) he was smoking and 2) when he put out the cigarette he gave way to the following gesture as he went on noting the development of the EVENT: he placed two fingers, fore- and middle, on his temple. This gesture signified an equable quizzicalness in the face of his own COMPULSION/CRAVING and/or the EVENT that presumably was COMPULSION/CRAVING'S endpoint. Through the gesture he held himself aloof from COMPULSION/CRAV-ING, or rather (X, or rather, Y), from the likely correspondence between COMPULSION/CRAVING and EVENT. I looked around: sometimes the configuration of PARTICIPANTS, though I preferred, I begged, to think of them as SPECTATORS just as I was a SPECTATOR, was menacing, sometimes not. In other words, they were massed in unison, sometimes not. Their

159

unison was a function purely of their numbers though it is disappointing to trace menace to so forthright and banal a parameter, but so be it. In order to profit from what I had come for my only hope was to become affected by—swept up into—the VIRULENCE of EVENT—as a SPECTATOR—always as a SPECTATOR—before being driven to depart by the massed menacing configuration. He moved over a seat and I became afraid that he was about to manifest his EXCITEMENT in a way that would prove my faith ill-founded. I anticipated a course of ACTIVITY that was defintively against the grain of two fingers placed on a temple. However, I am not sure my man gave way or had moved over even with an eye to the ACTIVITY that would instantly disqualify him for *semblable* status. He may have moved over merely to see better even if there was nobody that I could make out obstructing his vision directly in front. I tried to forget him and concentrate on EVENT. I had to believe the performers were performing minimally, that whatever was forced out of them was at the mercy of desire and aimed at connecting them each with his particular target. Inflection is crucial and alone betrays the shamelessness, the uncalculating calculation of authentic desire, indifferent to SPECTATOR and from whose vaporous sphere SPECTATOR must disappear. It is impossible to determine what is rehearsed, what the simple, therefore maximally VIRULENT, outpouching of desire since both simulation and authentic desire grasp what is nearest to hand or to inner thigh, that is to say, ready-made phrases tinged with bravado and unlocalizable denigration masking/flaunting raw want.

At moments I was completely given up to the EVENT, the EVENT in its VIRULENCE, as we speak of the potato in its skin or the pig in its blanket, to such an extent that my man was obliterated with comparable completeness. At a certain moment, as opposed to an uncertain one, the EVENT slowed, was slow in coming back, had faded out, died. One SPECTATOR cried out that somebody should act to ensure that EVENT went on following in the footsteps of

EVENT. Another cried back,"Why don't you complain if you're so impatient?" so that undeniably—what with the use of the word *impatient* under such conditions of stressful COMPULSION/CRAVING—what with the overall civility of the exchange—there was a strange beauty to such an incident kept sedately within bounds. Once EVENT resumed, or rather (X, or rather, Y), resumed its appearance of a smooth flow since appearances notwithstanding the EVENT had never ceased, (still another?) SPECTATOR contended that he who was responsible for managing the flow had been off making a telephone call. "Why doesn't he do that kind of thing in a..." (site servicing more widespread COMPULSION/CRAVINGS) . Once again, there was a strange beauty in the outcry as it strove to rally PARTICIPANTS, no, SPECTATORS, to a fervor with respect to their common heritage in opposition to a heritage out there where the call was made, the heritage of broad daylight, every day, of every other body's days. There was a strange beauty in this artless acceptation—conveyed through equally artless exasperation—of the EVENT'S anomalousness and, fleetingly rending the tissue of anonymity of which EVENT was constituted, anomalousness of belonging to the EVENT. There was a kind of affirmation here, of needs such as theirs were, such as theirs had turned out to be. For as long as the echo of the affirmation lasted (vying with EVENT'S soundtrack for my attention) there was no longer any shame in belonging to this group:The group had just been named in its anomalousness by a one of the group, inside the group, who naming also was outside the group, demonstrating that it was possible while very much inside to come outside the group and its urgency, and vice-versa, and therefore be undiagnosably inside and outside the urgency at the very same moment. The outcry showed that the crier therefore any crier had the courage to name and thereby transform the group no longer localizable as target of naming. And then the EVENT overcame once again with a VIRULENCE and it no longer mattered what anybody said. My

161

primary problem was how to hold/hold on to/contend with/the VIRULENCE of EVENT as it unfolded and beyond its unfolding. The only viable technique for holding/not holding on to the VIRULENCE is a devirulizing one. In actual fact, as opposed to virtual fact, I did not in the least wish to hold on to the VIRULENCE, I wanted to have done with VIRULENCE. But I refused then and there to submit to the only effective devirulizing technique, something like a point of honor. This devirulization technique holds the VIRULENCE in question before the mind's eye until the devirulizing, prodded, guided, goaded, by the VIRULENCE, has played itself out. And even if it is only the ACTIVITY that has played itself out and not the VIRULENCE per se, as if by contamination the VIRULENCE too is somehow attenuated. The most advanced devirulization technique, in other words (X, in other words, Y), the one I am most prone to practice but not in public, requires conscientious performance of the devirulizing activity in the strict absence of any specific upsurge of VIRULENCE, the performer therefore not waiting as usual for the VIRULENCE to assault but going out and expropriating said VIRULENCE before it can cohere much less assault.

To summon forth VIRULENCE in the absence of COMPULSION/-CRAVING and yoke it to the devirulizing activity obliged to play itself out to the bitter end truly is to triumph over EVENT. Along these lines, every nook and cranny normally susceptible to VIRULENCE is scoured in advance, proleptically, as it were, so that at the moment of unexpected inopportune therefore ghastly susceptibility the VIRULENCE mercilessly devolving upon the COMPULSION/CRAVING is hoist by its own petard, rendered null and void. Along similar lines, I tend to tell the stories of my life well in advance of their unfolding out there so as to eliminate the need to—erect the impossibility of living them. Having from time to time an obscure yet blinding premonition of that complete concept of myself supposedly comprising all that has happened, is happening, and will happen to said self I make it a point to disgorge the happenings so as blithely to foil their development now reduced to a mere anile aping of my augurs and therefore supremely distasteful to the entrepreneurs of such a development.

In short, to engage in the devirulizing ACTIVITY in the absence of all palpable enslavedness to VIRULENCE—not in its presence as I had suspected, probably unjustly, my man of doing—is the key, but to what. Noting the mounting interest to which my spectatorship was giving rise, to say nothing (to say nothing...) of the almost panting curiosity with which I fixed on that of my man, I was beginning to suspect, however reluctantly, that what initially I had taken for EVENT might in fact not be EVENT but the pretext for EVENT as the sum, nay, the product, of the interrelation of all SPECTATORS now PARTICIPANTS. The biggest stumbling block was being overcome: I was compelled to recognize that I, however anonymous, however invisible, however inconceivable, constituted a significant part of the EVENT, at least for some others. Homologically, the two fingers poised deftly on an inquiring temple were not outside vantage on but part and parcel of EVENT. From the point of view of some other(s) surely my fastidious SPEC-TATORSHIP was equivalent to the most robust participation in EVENT independent of whether or not they were aware—and even if aware how could they undergo in such a way that undergoing would be registered as an intersubjectively valid component of EVENT—that I had come and was continuing to come a very long way in my conception of EVENT's VIRULENCE. From their vantage within I did not have to be apprenticed to such a strenuously evolving conception of EVENT's VIRULENCE (where all the superfluity that had initially constituted indispensable accessories of VIRULENCE was being sheared toward a degree zero of EVENT as it turned out violating all my preestablished canons of VIRULENCE) to be, once again from their vantage within, always from their vantage, *of* the EVENT. They did not have to know what was going on unverifiably within, namely, a dawning of the consciousness that the so-called accessories were no longer vital and nothing more than obscurations of EVENT in its nudity indistinguishable from the acme of VIRULENCE — they did not have to know all this in order to live me as a PARTICIPANT in the EVENT.

I had determined my man, followed him in, he who had seduced the SITE for me, thereby sparing me the tedium-laden toying with vigilance preparatory to ingress. I had followed him in, sure he would be one knowing how to behave, that is to say (X, that is to say, Y), how to be always steering supremely clear of some ACTIVITY identifiable with PARTICIPATION. But now I was totally at sea regarding PARTICIPATION. From my purlieus I myself was PARTICIPATING. Completely on the margin of doing no doubt I myself was in some way contributing to the excitement, even the jouissance, of others. Might it even be true that the more marginal my locus the more I swelled the ranks of that jouissance. But I have taught myself to suspect such constructions—cement substance of stories, stories, stories—that deviating from the syntax of reality go on to parasitize the syntactic laissez-faire of their own anti-realm. I went back to the two fingers on his temple. The gesture still bespoke a bemused involvement. I observed and observed until it was clear that I was fascinated less, far less, by the SPECTACLE/ EVENT than by the remote possibility (less by X than by Y)— given all that the formal beauty of the gesture suggested of a handsel toward rarefactions even more exquisite—that he, generator of inexhaustible rarefactions, should comprehend such a SPECTACLE/EVENT. The firm foundation in inconceivability—given his exquisiteness as a gesture machine—yielding nonetheless to a gradual impalpable growth of comprehension was more exciting than the SPECTACLE/EVENT itself. How could such a SPECTACLE/EVENT begin to excite somebody like this, apotheosized by two fingers poised against the bulkhead of a bemused temple. Yes, yes, yes, you might think it was a simple case of his having all along been earmarked to embody the part of myself that stood back with wonder and incomprehension from the other's too rapid spontaneous animal distraint of VIRULENCE in ACTIVITY of a certain bruised sort. Here was the first red-blooded, red-handed proof that the EVENT as the sum of interrelations among all spectators was more than a literary fiction. For what had suddenly overcome me with its VIRULENCE was not the EVENT, that is to say (X, that is to say, Y) what initially I had taken to be the EVENT, but that EVENT's ability to generate virulence for somebody like him. Yes, yes, yes, simply he was enacting my buried and immediately available drama of a dawning of conscious avowal of certain, as opposed to uncertain, tastes. The EVENT did not excite. His possible comprehension of the EVENT's VIRULENCE excited. He looked around and around and around, discreetly of course. For a moment I feared he might be envious of the ACTIVITY, devirulizing or not, taking place circumambiently, in which case he was no longer any man of mine and must be jettisoned for betraying my faith, to wit (X, to wit, Y), the certainty that he had come, like me, for SPECTATORSHIP and not for PARTICIPATION, not for ACTIVITY. But he was only looking around at what was to be seen, as opposed to what wasn't, and wasn't I guilty of the same lapse even, especially, at this very moment of condemning his. But for me looking around was less a definable activity, I mean, ACTIVITY, than a kind of loophole in ACTIVITY, a momentary dive into nonbeing for purposes of recruitment through self-terrorization. I was afraid he would initiate some ACTIVITY, devirulizing or not, with himself or another, that would remove him completely from the benign influence of the protocol that was our sole bond. That would be as good as abandoning me. In other words, as long as he was forever on the verge of playing out my latent drama of a dawning of the consciousness of the VIRULENCE to be had here for the asking he was my man still. Then he got up and left. I knew I too had now to leave. Entering had not been a matter of choice, rather the abolition of not merely the gamut of conceivable choices but the conceivability of choice itself, castration of the possibility of choice.

What was departure? I intended to set out after him but before I could begin a hooded figure tried to bar my passage to the exit. I think he touched me, I think he pricked my middle finger. At first the sky was completely overcast except, in the southwesterly distance, for a brief span of blue in whick a peak of cumulus frothed which blue frothing suggested and confirmed that when I looked back, as I was sure to do, on this walk it would be nostalgia but for something very strictly speaking outside the walk itself, a distant prospect of what the walk might have been if circumstances ever went right with this world. In other words, I immediately saw, or rather, smelled (X, or rather, Y), that this was not to be the walk outlined in the mythic vision of my life as a venerable succession, less a succession than (less A than B) an imbrication impossible to ravel out, of story events in their primordial perfection, but rather, (not P, but rather, Q), a constant battle between such mythic embodiments of perfection and that perfection's imperfect realization which, it was clear, sponsored and perpetuated what was nothing more ultimately than a parasitizing caricature of fuller-bodied stouter-hearted avatars. All I knew was that the sky was not blue and was therefore incapable of casting ferns, pine needles, squirrel dung, in the requisite mythic true light. As it had been out of the question to relieve myself at the SITE whence I had just emerged pricked, goaded, contaminated, I was weighted down with toxic materials and understandably could not give full attention to the landscape. Instead of following the road—his—that was clearly leading, past pine forests and beechen groves, to town, I ended up on a tributary skirting the edge of the cliffs, sailing boats cozily nesting in the tranquil wide bay they overhung.

Past the cyclists I made my way on even smaller paths that to judge by the bodiless heads of distant stragglers belonged to an infinitely ramifying network completely swallowed up in gorse, ferns, butter-cups and stonecrop. Coming eventually to a cove where the shelves of rock were for some distance down virtually horizontal there I pissed and having pissed unobserved was now in a position to lie down on one such shelf and sleep, united under the sun's rays to the kingdoms animal, vegetable, and above all mineral I had just irrigated so prodigally. Finally I came to a little port just as he was departing by a kind of ghat, the two fingers still or once more poised on the worrisome temple. It was clear from a new inflection of the gesture that the little port accessible by helicopter or ghat vastly tormented and depressed him. His receding buttocks put the finishing touches on a surmise that, so I was now discovering, alternately ravaged and exalted me. So that once he was out of sight it was only natural I should be eager to visit. I studied it first from high above, a little white house of god on my left, the obligatory couple sitting in bathing suits on a bench before the tiny edifice quickly rising presumably to resume their leisurely loverly walk with arms entangled around each other's naked waist. I assumed I had interrupted some amorous nibbling, at genitalia or worse. I descended the steep to the port and found the same couple in front of me, noting also that a well-dressed man seated at a table in what looked at first glance like the port's only outdoor bar/restaurant/-nightclub/amusement park was casting furtive glances at the couple's male, moustached and seemingly very much at home in his maleness. At moments the sun was very hot until a chilling breeze all at once penetrated to the very skin my many layers of clothing, driving me to don yet another that rendered me when all was said and done just as—even more—just as, just as—susceptible. I sat on a wall at the very edge of the green water. The constrictedness of this port with its sun beating down proclaimed an idyll. I climbed up as I had climbed down and resumed my promenade from cove to cove, each descending precariously to the sea, bluegreen in spots, otherwise black from sunstroke. But no matter how far I roamed I knew I had to return to that port where I had caught sight of him tackling the ghat, his receding buttocks taut with manly resignation. Back at the port I immediately understood that before I saw the port I had seen that the port tormented and unmanned him and so there was an exhilaration, understandable if not commendable, in having this preestablished relation to fall back on, this barrier to

167

overcome, should I, as I had done, return. I basked, for the port was for the time being synonymous with my penetrating glimpse of his reaction to it, it was nothing more than his reaction to it, and so my reaction, with so much at hand to deform, could only be new, unique, and daring, a challenge to whatever his flagging sensibility had determined to be the law of the port. His relation to the port, such as I had seized it, was now a dead relation, spread out before me and only waiting to be reviled, that is to say (X, that is to say, Y) rehabilitated by my living vibrant counterrelation, vibrant, I had to admit—before another made me admit it—precisely, as opposed to imprecisely, because another, namely, he, had already done all the dirty work of rendering a relation to such an entity conceivable. He had civilized the port, simple as that, given it a coherence against which my likes was now permitted luxuriously to react, against which canvassing and cavilling to publish the brummagem daring of my own special brand of refutation so what if ultimately and elementally parasitic on some other's—this other's—his—anterior upsurge. So what if my exhilaration, published or not, subsisted only in relation to his grief. Basking ever basking and stripped down now to one or two layers I refused to consider how much of this exhilaration if exhilaration indeed it was was exhilaration over the port itself and how much buttock-thrusting at being at last in a position to react against his—somebody's—anybody's—his—warm throbbing nakedly exposed core of prior reaction. I did not have to evict this crude and futile preoccupation from my skull, it never gained admittance. Very quickly I was tiring of this port, of all ports, of this port, now I had succeeded in paying him back for the exquisite beauty of a gesture that had been the keenest rebuke imaginable to my own formless panic at some unlocalizable moment in the remote past. Finding myself wishing to come to the end of all ports, I cut off toward a plantation, took the wrong road and ended up pursued by the barking of what turned out to be a harmless little dog yet with another, that might I might point out have been much larger, furnishing invisible support in a background denuded of all greenery, cut across the field, took the right road at last.

In its cemetery before one of the very first row graves but not as one come to mourn stood an inquisitive tourist peering, he. Passing I made a point of farting low, as one speaks of lying low, I was and am not sure he heard it, and if he did, now I was passed, to what could he ascribe it. On I walked, caught in the rain, cursing my fate as sent me in the form of a rainstorm, cursing the road back once again impossible to locate in that unbounded rete of fields despite the bellowing signpost of tourists converging just like him on ruins of particular interest, the proliferation of cars, motorbikes, bicycles, scooters, imminence of a sunburst in east or west, imminent prospect of a warm bed and a polite if not quite civil welcome from my hosts from whom I intended at all costs to conceal my unspeakable abstention from ACTIVITY at a site of whose existence, that is to say, of whose unspeakability, they were in all probability completely unawares. Regarding them through their bedroom window—the archetypical couple in front of the television where the speaker's head, larger, oh so very much larger, than either, in arbitrating their purest absence of a relation was turning out to be far more important than the relation itself—I decided to move on. Despite such details in which the subsequent stages of the journey were certain to abound I could only despair that the triumph of having positively adored the port that he had with such cavalier glumness left for dead was by now worn off. Dogs went on barking in the distance, the road made unwieldy turns taking me always further and further from any prospect of a sunburst, there were few cars, only blood, sorrow of a life ill-lived and what I could only designate, suddenly it came to me, as my PLIGHT. This was what it meant to be plighted, consigned to the innards of a PLIGHT.

I walked on, tempted at every puny crossroads to return to the steeps and stepwise descent of their shelves, to stand fast on one such shelf as the gulls molting screeched overhead, flying wildly as they screeched, shadows flaying the funnel-shaped dive into the belly of noon. As I advanced one gull emitted a four-noted signal or did I imagine it, did I have to imagine it in order to have something to pivot on or against since he had not responding first beat me a path to the gulls, commented with a shrug of his buttock on their flayed screeching, their shadowy contamination of the unmolting landscape. I could not adore the gulls as I had adored the port, or rather (A, or rather, B), as I had adored the possibility of adoring the port in the face of his shrugged despondent departure, for my adoration of A, B, or C was and could never be anything but his prior despair—but with the sign reversed—in the face of that A, B, or C. His anteriority was the form and substance of my present. It would be to profane savagely the memory of meaning to say, as I am tempted now to say but will not say: This is why only to him could I speak of the PLIGHT.

I had no trouble finding him. Only in the vicinity of the port had he proved elusive and that elusiveness probably had more to do with my midday torpor than with his shiftiness. "And how did everything go with the anti-PLIGHT?" This, he explained, was how he must refer to my visit to the SITE. "When the thugs mounted in the back I knew I had to leave." He said, "They might have been there, be there still, to minister to the needs of certain regulars whose needs, evidently, are not your needs." "I thought they could very easily take it into their heads to block my passage and so I leaped up and made for the exit." "You almost, in so doing, knocked me down." "But just as quickly a hooded figure made for me and muttering something unintelligible poked me with a forefinger. I was immediately contaminated. I am still contaminated." "In other words, you have reached that point, long sought, whence you can no longer allow yourself anything resembling human contact lest you infect the innocent." How well you understand, my eyes shone. Anticipating he added: "Don't worry: I know this is not the PLIGHT itself. This is simply the busy doings of the anti-PLIGHT. Did you always dread being touched." Without waiting for a reply: "Now you have a good reason not to be touched, not to touch. Bravo." Before I could reply he said:"Did you not fly from the PLIGHT"—how easily he brought himself to speak of the PLIGHT but wasn't I simply getting a taste of my own anti-medicine: my naming, of the PLIGHT, was providing him with a foothold in subsequent naming as defaming. But had I in fact named the PLIGHT at any point in our dealings so far?—"to the SITE where first we met precisely because it, the PLIGHT, divulged you as one who had been touched and was capable however reluctantly of touching in return and who, if said PLIGHT is to be resolved, must go on touching. So that this new obsession with contamination and its obligatory tabulation of signs and symptoms, is it anything more than your way of holding on to a body you must otherwise abjure, in the face, I mean, of its dissolution compliments of a PLIGHT patched together only to rob you of yourself, scuttle all footholds, shred your sails, batter your binnacle, send you foundering beyond appeal at the wily whim of chance and the briny hour." He looked off, to underline, I think, an absence of coercion above and far beyond what the words already published of such an absence. I looked off to underline that the anti-PLIGHT embodied no such stratagem, that is to say, nothing that stank of choice but was on the contrary and preeminently an escape from matters of choice, a sabbath from the hard labor of choosing celebrated at a SITE *no different from any other* and without further ado inaugurated with the maimed rite of pacing back and forth before said SITE in order just before entering to stake out the moment of minimal conspicuity. "But," he began, looking as if he was on the verge of lashing out, "what if all this fussy pacing back and forth, back and forth, is in fact designed to induce conspicuity even if such conspicuity means nothing less than obliteration for isn't—listening carefully, chum— such obliterating collision with respectable tongue clickers loitering on the margin of your obloquy ultimately for all its promised horror and when you come right down to it far less tormenting than lonely COMPULSION/CRAVING achieving its exitus unimpeded and unchecked. Therefore, you don't nor will you ever come to know yourself in that COMPULSION/CRAVING for isn't it always the case that suddenly swept up into its maelstrom and therefore most estranged from your preponderant sidewalk self you generally find yourself more than for SATIATION hungering after confirmation of your continued existence beyond all the ravages of said

171

maelstrom. And better than any rubber stamp the blind and blundering gaze of respectful folk serrating the edge of the SITE furnishes just the confirmation you need, that is to say, a parody of confirmation feeding off the craved verdict of contaminatedness which verdict is of course horrific yet strangely familiar and infinitely more reassuring than to find yourself adrift and immune, immune and adrift, in a sea of imminent SATIATION. I speak of course of the SATIATION that has for accomplice two fingers and that temple south of the belly..." He bracketed the hopelessness of my incomprehension with a sighing look right between my eyes. "If only you could begin to understand that far more terrifying than infectedness is unmitigated SATIATION then I might begin to believe you will live to combat and vanquish the PLIGHT. But you are very far from beginning to conceive that SATIATION without let is far more terrifying than all this rigamarole about flagitious hooded figures seceding from a configuration of thuglike janissaries barring egress with the sole intent of infecting through touch." I wanted to get away from the hooded figure, mine, now his, far more his than mine. Yet I did not want to come back to the PLIGHT. I did not expect him to say: "What did you do inside. You obviously saw what I did. What did you do."

ffective immediately promoted assistant creative vice assets XXXXXX double the free repair period our team of seasoned twenty-four hour toll a smooth-satin traditional charm functional beauty handrubbed eleven times hi-tech modular breathtaking hiss laser-produced index search P-Mount dampened low-mass tonearm gravy ladle plugging your camcorder right to cancel by special arrangement encased in a clear acrylic dynamic leather adventure in fashion tapered panel stitching sleek stunningly different personal statement run your finger crossover network racy casual sportive dash change personalities extended laminate no more rechargeable vacuum foyer, dining room, den, as well accent for the executive bold contemporary reflection two-way speakerphone every muscle group affordable at home detachable pullstrap snap-proof rugged without being calorie consumption readout microprocessor pamper someone special picture ejection

He took it all in, every last bloody detail, sighed, said, "So after all we have said and all I have tried to prove you go on insisting this, your SITE, is just like any other SITE and that the transactions taking place all around you—us—the ACTIVITY without caesura—was in fact unacceptably atypical of comportment at such a SITE. You still refuse to believe the ACTIVITY of those ostensible offenders, hooded or unhooded, is perfectly acceptable at a SITE purposefully erected to aid and abet such ACTIVITY. For, I more than suspect, if you were to admit that such a SITE is deliberately destined for the perpetration of such ACTIVITY then the fissure between you and the world of lolling bystanders is irrevocably widened. As if it can be widened any more than it is irrevocably widened." "I refuse." "Yes, and reading between the lines of all you have just disgorged I can see why you refuse. Direness of your commitment to ACTIVITY at the SITE is certainly rendered more urgent when you accept the purposefulness of the SITE. At the present time your EXCITEMENT springs less from what you do than from what you see and far less from what you see than from undergoing over and over and over again the inconceivability of envisaging your own possible PARTICIPATION in or enactment of that seen. But enactment must remain as inconceivable as the horror of contaminatedness being ultimately less horrible then undeviating and unmolested ACTIVITY in quest of SATIATION." Stupidly—I could taste the stupidity—I proclaimed: "I don't really believe in the hooded figure's power to contaminate. All along I have been tormented less by the real possibility of infection than by my unsolicited capacity to subsidize that possibility in defiance of common sense. If you must know, in encountering the hooded figure I was tormented less by him than by the overwhelming fecundity of an exertion in behalf of turning myself into one by him contaminated beyond repair. And how marvelous that he should have been so providentially placed to meet my dread more than halfway." "And I could say: How marvelous that you were so providentially placed—outside the cemetery, I mean—to assail me

173

and thereby contaminate me irretrievably through your volley of farts." In a more didactic vein: "It seems to me you must always have dreaded simple contact as contamination but only within a SITE set apart—despite all your spectatorly protestations to the contrary—for ACTIVITY of a certain type—yes, set apart—were you able to give birth at last to that dread. And contaminatedness is of course inextricably bound up with a sense of irrevocability. Might I even go so far as to say the contaminatedness is the irrevocability, the mere pretext for a horrified sense of irrevocable apartness. But I maintain that this horrified sense of apartness is a mitigation compared to the simple sense of self that must devolve upon you in accepting the apartness of the SITE. The question becomes of course what the horrified sense of irrevocability does for you." He waited. I, too, found myself waiting. We both waited. Then: "It estranges me from the PLIGHT, it spares my having to tell the story of the PLIGHT. If before the PLIGHT was a source of horror now an even greater source of horror—yes, even greater—is my contaminatedness so that it is only natural that beatifically estranged from the PLIGHT that is I I am suddenly afflicted with nostalgia for the relatively more innocuous horror of a PLIGHT that is no longer I, not even remotely in the vicinity of that I." As if reading diagonally down a scrawled fever chart he intoned: "Resettled then amid the purlieus of a horror far greater than that brandished by the PLIGHT—namely, that brandished by the anti-PLIGHT generated at *the* SITE no different from any other—you allow a cornfed nostaligia to row you back to the PLIGHT itself but as other than itself, to wit, the promised land of instant retrospect." "As far as I am concerned with respect, in time, to any moment x, any previous moment, x - epsilon, where epsilon may be as infinitesimal as you wish, precisely and solely because previous, is necessarily bathed in an inaccessible luster of enviable novelty and painlessness. The PLIGHT/anti-PLIGHT distinction brings this dialectical tension to fever pitch."

Very kindly, as is the way of such men, just when I was about to

174

take what appeared to be the beginning of a long long silence for official endorsement of what I hoped must appear as my somber refusal to further examine the difficulties now facing me sideways, all subsumable under this rubric PLIGHT—endorsement that had to be founded on the firmest of convictions, namely, that everything would turn out all right, better than all right, if for no otner reason than to indemnify the excessiveness, though this time completely forestalled, of my tendency to exacerbate through worry—just when I had begun to take his earnest of a long long silence for seasoned endorsement of this wholehearted refusal of my PLIGHT, or rather, of the reality of that PLIGHT, he announced timidly that perhaps, in order to waylay its impending burden, I might look into some SIDELINES.

I fought back but hopelessly, within the newly hatched context of a fait accompli, that of the PLIGHT as in one fell stroke conceived, brought to birth, and nurtured through infancy to adult monstrosity. I told him SIDELINES required too much electioneering. He backed off, kindly, though less, so it seemed, from fear of my rage than of his own reactant warmth polluting the purity of the rehabilitation SITE. Yet this backing off was even more terrifying for it implied authentic surprise, tactfully suppressed, that I was not spontaneously embracing every such opportunity to thwart annihilation, by, in, the PLIGHT. "So the MAIN LINE comes first." Reproaching me with a certain, as opposed to an uncertain, incredulity he instantaneously created my MAIN LINE, better yet the unassailable integrity of a MAIN LINE whose requirements were as it turned out—according, that is, to his incredulity's conception, in other words, construction, of my misconception—at war with those of the PLIGHT. And simultaneously with the MAIN LINE's creation I found myself astonished and enraged that even at this late date it was still—even at this late date—it was still, the MAIN LINE, I mean—a matter to be clarified, a commodity to be vended, or rather (P, or rather, P'), a commodity with a history to be vended. At this late date—at this late date—so what if concurrent with its totally unforeseen and instantaneous creation—there should have been absolutely no doubt that

175

the MAIN LINE came first even if deep down I wanted to be rescued from the MAIN LINE or rather (A, or rather, B) from a newly expanding immemorially stagnant fidelity to this concept of a MAIN LINE coming first before everything for mightn't such fidelity turn out to be more depleting than the MAIN LINE itself or than sober confrontation of the PLIGHT hovering or lurking somewhere in its distance, definable alternately as MAIN LINE's mammoth foreground and infinitely receding depth. Yet I also knew, or began to know, or at least suspected, or rather, the MAIN LINE itself was beginning to suspect in the manner, that is, proper to a MAIN LINE, that the hunger to drown the MAIN LINE was by no means incompatible with its flowering. Though a statement of this kind—"So the MAIN LINE comes first"— mewling its need for clarification could very well be a tactical ploy and first step in the direction of uprooting me from an engagement at once too total and too substanceless given the urgency coming from another direction. Prompting me to state that in point of fact the MAIN LINE was my first concern he was hoping the statement itself in the shape of its caricatural echoes could cure me of the gratuitous and absurd infirmity it struggled to bring into being. XXX The sun XXX XXXX XXXX X
In the face of this new outburst he backed off. I was a bit baffled for I could not quite imagine anybody, especially him, intimidated by a rage that was unmistakably an heuristic specimen deployed purely for his, my mentor's, benefit in fortifying me to overcome the PLIGHT in which I was sure to agree never again to believe once it was safely overcome.
ansnans ansnan dnsnd788s dnsnd s8930475
At the same time, for all these massive motions and even more paroxysmal threats of motion, I could not leave, had to stay on, begging for refutation of my PLIGHT, or rather, of what his unwelcome solicitude sketched of that PLIGHT's sinuosity. I needed to find out if I was indeed doomed without a SIDELINE, his SIDELINE, or if introduction of this concept of SIDELINE had been a response not to the PLIGHT itself but only to my own

panicked exaggerated construction of that PLIGHT (not to X but only to Y). I dared to think never would he have dared to suggest a SIDELINE if for the PLIGHT in its nudity, that is to say, a non-PLIGHT, I had not substituted an anathema-laden figurehead apotropaically ornamented with springes, deadfalls, culs-de-sac and consequently ripe for refutation. So that after all and at last it was within the bounds of probability to view his acumen as addressing infinitely less the PLIGHT than a maimed parody. If I managed once and for all to subdue the extremeness of my constructions couldn't I plausibly look forward to shelving all counsel, his and everybody else's, as no longer relevant to anything outside the pale of those constructions.

HSHDHSHD less clouds skdksk 2637273 bns less clouds ememrm toilet to your right

Still I could not leave for it was no longer only a question of having the PLIGHT refuted but of remaining in the vicinity of its supreme dragoman lest I risk ambush by its, the PLIGHT's, emissaries coming regularly to meet him halfway. Propinquity to the PLIGHT, then, could be tolerated only as subliminal parasitization of his infinitely ramifying vision of its essence, that is to say, of its refusal to go away unslaked. "You are convinced," he ventured, "these extreme formulations are a mere apotropaic device streamlined to elicit my cataplasmic amusement at their *outrance*. The apotropaically extreme formulation leads to obliteration—its own of course, and the PLIGHT's in tandem. The PLIGHT becomes no more than a function, that is to say (A, that is to say, B), a phantom of your extreme formulation of what you strive to pawn off as its essence. Yet in some very basic sense, it, THE PLIGHT, precedes, succeeds and surrounds, and from deep within burrows toward trituration of that extreme formulation."

Hahaha handsel sndnsn dnsndnsnd dish of XXX touch

Despite the totally unexpected show of kindness still I could not budge for the not so simple reason that I had come to hate him for singlehandedly creating the lucid contour of my refusal to budge the MAIN LINE from its eternal resting place, that is to say, its trysting place with eternity, thereby implying that I had, and at every moment waking and unwaking, some sort of choice with respect to the priority I assigned it. Even if in fact I knew no small part and parcel of the potency of the MAIN LINE's unctuous charm, above all things terrestrial and connubial, etc., must be its knowing usurpation—and at every moment and in every situation and in the name of a potentiality at the very least problematical—of all other choices instantaneously and mercilessly relegated to the tundra of embryos. In my eyes only choicelessness seems to hold out the prospect of salvation, makes me beautiful. For choice implying a conscious striving toward what is best for oneself is therefore an acceptance of that self's legitimate craving to flourish and of the inevitability of tactful rejection of those selves that do not subserve, through no fault of their own—there's the pathos—this quest for the best. How explain that what most pained was not outright destruction or arrant cruelty but this tactful rejection of this or that in the name of the other. I gambled: "The moment of choice implies the healthful affirmation of the self especially legible in the look of wounded longing from those not chosen. The moment of choice erects the primacy of the self's voyage toward a reasonable fulfillment which voyage necessarily subsidizes the separateness of self from self. When, at the SITE, I chose your gesture (two fingers on temple) over all others all those others were cast aside as insalubrious to my evolution. But of course I was so overwhelmed by its formal beauty that there was no question of a choice among choices with its concomitant mercilessness of repudiation. Therefore I hurt nobody and still belong to everybody. This is why I am still beautiful." "Your beauty then," he spewed, "is nothing but this masked, camouflaged, and dissimulated choice of what you crave but as if it has chosen you in a frenzy of vindictiveness, as if it is being forced down the gullet of your saintly striving to be everybody's friend, helpmate, lover. Your beauty, so-called, is this abstention from actively choosing what is good or VIRULENT lest

178

you be obliged concurrently to choose yourself and as being apart from other beings, that is to say, your self-interest as a fact of life as neutral as shitting, pissing or indulging in that ACTIVITY indissolubly favored by a SITE amid whose functional amenities we first laid eyes each on the other. For I was as conscious of your gesture as you of mine.'' Then

Deferred obligation to purchase XXXX Team of seasoned specialists sbdbsd desires the customer's rugged durability *ten* extra broad gussets when you acquire exclusive condom cigarette Sound that attains uprecedented depths of simulated richness Double cassette deck Direct-drive audio-return turntable

What with the offer of the cigarette and its refusal and on the part of both parties the nauseated effort to simulate a benevolent unconsciousness of all that had failed to transpire it was clear that he had omitted miserably to honor the well-nigh numinous intensity of my dedication to the MAIN LINE. I was relieved not to have enumerated in even greater detail than I had that numinous intensity for to enumerate is to make conceivable, therefore fungible, therefore easily obliterated. It was at that very moment with the cigarette strewn somewhere between us and the moon rising somewhere in the windowpane, that I took it upon myself at last to ponder those factors in his own life that could compel him not to see me as definitely yoked and as by divine decree to the MAIN LINE's priority. ''From what I can gather you in earliest youth must Money nothing enriches your home better than exquisitely handicrafted, mass-market XXX We have all been faced with the unexpected guests serving space kettle of fish)S)S)D)D Please notice your toll-free lovely parquetry top must arrive with its fluted legs adrift for easier shipment but the screws VAV-SHAHDJS the screws AMSMAMDMSM wonder how you ever managed without YYYY classic yet class SY easy-to-assemble double density from coordinate upholstery the free 15-month examination. Suddenly, I wanted, now that I had completely disgorged it, whatever I had concocted in the way of depiction to be far more revealing of me than of him. More than to dazzle with omniscience I wanted my depic-

179

tion, however unprecedented, to trap me into the shabbiest and therefore the most curative self-revelation. Surely this portrait, this depiction I had just visited upon him still had time to turn out to be the datum crucial to an understanding at last of why I went on resisting and resisting and resisting *his* depiction, even more curative, of my PLIGHT. Surely I had just painted his willfully insufficient understanding of my allegiance, numinous or otherwise, to the priority of the MAIN LINE with too lurid and garish a palette for the disjunction between portrait and model not to be far wider than that between portrait and portraitist. Initially propelled by a conviction, when it came to my LINE, of *his* pathologic myopia, acting on this conviction hopefully I had managed, when it came down to necessary—yes, absolutely necessary, I saw it now—repudiation of inane allegiance to said LINE's priority with its accessory decimation of concerns far more vital, namely, PLIGHT's lasting overthrow, to alert him only to my own. "You are desperate," he remarked, "to sustain the fiction that PLIGHT can only stand in the way of MAIN LINE. According to you, the latter's raw materials or semi-raw can only be assimilated through some processus akin to extended contemplation whereas in actual fact (X whereas in actual fact Y) you tend to perceive, ingest, assimilate all you need and then some in no more than a split second. Conceivably, then, you are no amateur when it is a question of tending to the PLIGHT's manifold exigencies while pimping in behalf of MAIN LINE's priority. You loathe this worthy talent and persist in striving to become other as prerequisite for MAIN LINE's beginning to begin. And though MAIN LINE has more than begun and on more than one occasion—in fact on every occasion—still you go on holding fast to this unachieved and fatuous prerequisite as if it is a very axiom of your existence, must become the very axiom of your existence if you are to exist at all. In other words, you will begin to exist, that is to say, as MAIN LINER, for is there any other existence worth having, only after you have transformed yourself into an other. When will you learn that the PLIGHT need not be an obstruction to contemplation but, threatening to uproot you from your ostensibly most fertile targets—when you are seated under the lindens staring into the shallows of a canal, for example—a source of dialectical enrichment. Take it from me, given what you are you will be able to extract whatever it is your kind extracts from sites like the canal only in the shadow of some ostensibly thwarting counter-vailing COMPULSION/CRAVING driving you toward a SITE deemed well in advance completely, profaningly, incompatible with this, the first and foremost, and scandalously sanctioning ACTIVITY that couldn't care less whether or not it flouts all the hoary principles on which said first and foremost is erected. Along the same lines as this belief in the fiction of an absolute need for extended contem-plation—if, that is, the MAIN LINE is to be nourished—lies your uncanny ability to confront each new situation, that is to say, each new flight from PLIGHT, in the guise of one pillaged to nullity in the realm of the spiritual in order that, dutifully convinced new situation or new absence of same is your lost hope, you may plausibly deliver yourself up to it utterly. Functioning then in the realm of the MAIN LINE depends from a series of fictions."

As I hovered over him with fists clenched he said, "Yes, by all means tell me the story of your life, all that might account for such an impasse declaiming before us now."

Began to rattle off XXX ancedotes shape, stay, home trial, shopping with confidence, tubular chrome steel frame, take nine months, perfect for leg and lower, hydraulic shocks, chain-driven flywheel, you and your family, privacy of your own

If he wanted a story I was still not his man. "Prefer details, I see," he said. In response to the queryingly querulous expression he refused to manifest I graciously added, "Only details, you must know, are resistant to the caricature of paraphrase, in other words, language, in other words, the denigration of language. Only details call a halt to language—to language, that is, getting even through paraphrase with language. Only details are scrawled in a language resistant to language. But don't get me wrong. When I am just setting out—as I did following you into the SITE set apart as is the way with such

SITES, no, no, no, set apart for nothing—but it never fails:.Every element indispensable to the story's mythic unfolding is undergone immediately as incompatible with, well-nigh overtly hostile to, such an unfolding. So is it any wonder that rather than act my story I prefer to witness the ACTIVITY of others." "Once long ago—"
tubular steel grid XXX
rebate plywood
YY diskette
"—you must have been forced to witness a fragment of the story of others. And you are still attempting to devirulize that ACTIVITY embodied in the fragment. And I daresay you were and are less excited by the fragment's inherent VIRULENCE than perplexed—to such a degree that perplexity became and remains the most potent form of EXCITEMENT—as to why you were called upon and so young to testify to such VIRULENCE, or worse, render virulent through blundering spectatorship. And so you are obliged to return over and over to the SITE, merely to witness. And so engrossed over and over do you become in witnessing—in order, of course, only to discover why once upon a time you were called upon to witness—that you cannot conceive of a life beyond witnessing, a life that could in contradistinction take advantage of the powerlessness of others in the face of their own witnessing, hunger to witness. Thus, your love of detail—fragment—anything that obliging you to bear witness permits the pretermission of your own eminently witnessable acts, to say nothing of the story their sequence suggests." "Whether I live or do not live the story's unfolding I do not want to have to talk about having lived it step by step. But don't take my lack of enthusiasm for loathing of the story itself, or rather (A, or rather, B), only of the story itself. It is the uttering I loathe, the encapsulation, in, by, language, and, to make matters worse, having once done my duty by language, the being understood. To utter is to give relative value to what is beyond value, thus to devalue

182

ın the marketplace of being, and so you can begin to understand my lack of enthusiasm for such self-devaluation. And of course you, the listener, take the lack of enthusiasm over the prospect of cowlike devaluation through language for lack of enthusiasm over act—story—myth in its nudity, which is of course there also. Now you must at any rate understand why I prefer the contextlessness of detail, detail digging deeper and deeper roots into the very absence of context, soil, bedrock." "Give me an example," said he.

selected for quality xx confidence months to swivel chair toll-free electronic brain that controls PM/AM audiovisual quartz synthesizer tuna, soft-touch noise reduction, 2000 channel cable-capable, billed to my PPP abdbab three teakwood GSHDHSHD deferred payment burgundy navy chartreuse wide zippered, top adjustable roomy, exceptional value, return it in original mouths to pay, feed no finance

He seemed more or less satisfied with my detail and its resistance to paraphrase. He nodded: "And clearly one more instance of injustice in a life riddled with same." I hung my head, hadn't been aware that once again I had allowed myself to run to him with yet another instance of all that had been perpetrated against my being as proof, proof, proof, but of what. "Perhaps you run to me—as you just did—I did provoke you this time, that *is* true—so exultantly with these instances, yes, look at you, exultantly, exultantly is the only word, because though you believe you revile them and the world that hatched them in point of fact you thrive insatiably on their proof of your innocence as a function of incessant punishment far far beyond the scope of your trespasses."

As I seemed unwilling either to confirm or deny he summed up as follows: "PLIGHT then is conducive to details born, I might go so far as to say, only under the pressure of PLIGHT. And these details, quickly shovelled into the maw of the MAIN LINE, what are they or rather what ratifies them if not and better than a sense of the injustice perpetrated against you which they dutifully

embody. In other words, now that we have come to the end of our road together you must ask—" "I ask nothing." "—if at this point you could be disembarrassed of the PLIGHT whether in point of fact you should want to be." In spite of myself I jumped in: "No, no, no, I would not want to be disembarrassed of the PLIGHT for I have already invested so much in its fantastical embellishment. From initial absolute rage at its insidious excrescence-like gratuitousness—like a snake out of Virgil—it has become, through that very rage, I mean, indistinguishable from my corpuscles and cement substance. But always, alas, only as a chimera subsidized by panic. And how I loathe myself—or the PLIGHT—no, myself, the PLIGHT is innocent after all—for generating this meaning. For in dredging up such a meaning for the delectation of two fingers poised on a temple—and what, after all, is such an allusion but one more obeisance to the machinations of meaning—what have I managed to do but allow myself to be sucked ever closer toward the earth where bastard meanings are encouraged to proliferate like wasps. Yet why do I look only on the dark side closer to earth: At any moment you might very well oblige me by admitting that the PLIGHT does not exist thereby giving official—for in your own quiet way you do stink of officialdom—recognition to my astounding windfall in being one encumbered with PLIGHT-bequeathed details at the service of flight from story as the failure of story but with absolutely nothing of that PLIGHT's plightfulness." "You yourself and nobody else are to blame for these meanings for though you came here seeming to be going quickly mad you were and at every step of the way—and I hardly blame you considering your host of other engagements—carefully titrating that madness, or rather, that capacity for madness, against a minute-by-minute capacity to tolerate same in behalf of the details toward which it might procure your exclusive privity."
How express love better than timelessly ¼ carat total weight
I marveled at how still he stood as I went about raging against my

absence of surprise at all he had just said and, so it now seemed, even more insidiously left unsaid, or rather (A, or rather, B), against the amiable ease with which—oh grossest betrayal imaginable of that weary old desideratum to be one who did not assimilate instantaneously and for all time but only as a result of weary old contemplation comprising centuries not necessarily terminating in assimilation of a single shred worth shredding—I assimilated all he said and left unsaid thereby confirming their plausibility or, at least, their conceivability.

gsgdhdh a different look for your each and every reflects and betrays your outstanding appreciation of non-winding dependability XXYY revolutionary wedge-shaped volume-control, velcro-hook, state of safeguard unauthorized access, multiplies and divides in the free world

So at last he was the one now raging, presumably at my refusal to blubberingly concur or at the exasperatingly amiable ease with which my unspeaking posture concurred in all he said and left unsaid. "Go," said he, finally. "Take refuge from the PLIGHT in more cowardly abstention from unspeakable ACTIVITY at unspeakable SITES like the one that conveniently arranged our first and last encounter. Stake it all out with your usual and now celebrated recoil from manly choice. (I marvel at the appalling rapidity with which you stake out these SITES merely, it quickly becomes apparent, through recoiling cowardice to cast aspersions on their usefulness in ministering to the sublimely legitimate COMPULSION/CRAVINGS of their habitués with whom you of course avow no kinship beyond the anemic and mutilated gaping that links SPECTATOR to PERFORMER.) Go, go, go, out of my sight, take refuge from PLIGHT, but by all means and at all costs avoid such gutter confrontations as might redound to the speedier resolution of that PLIGHT. Avoid the port, of course, it will only make you sad."

With no obligation to
plug
an auxiliary jack

185

Books from

FOUR WALLS EIGHT WINDOWS

Algren, Nelson. **NEVER COME MORNING.**

Anderson, Sherwood. **THE TRIUMPH OF THE EGG.**

Brodsky, Michael. **X IN PARIS.**

Brodsky, Michael. **XMAN.**

Codrescu, Andrei, ed. **AMERICAN POETRY SINCE 1970: UP LATE.**

Dubuffet, Jean.
ASPHYXIATING CULTURE AND OTHER WRITINGS.

Howard-Howard, Margo (with Abbe Michaels).
I WAS A WHITE SLAVE IN HARLEM.

Johnson, Phyllis, and Martin, David, Eds.
**FRONTLINE SOUTHERN AFRICA:
DESTRUCTIVE ENGAGEMENT.**

Null, Gary.
**THE EGG PROJECT:
GARY NULL'S COMPLETE GUIDE TO GOOD EATING.**

Santos, Rosario, ed.
**AND WE SOLD THE RAIN: CONTEMPORARY FICTION
FROM CENTRAL AMERICA.**

Sokolov, Sasha. **A SCHOOL FOR FOOLS.**

Wasserman, Harvey.
HARVEY WASSERMAN'S HISTORY OF THE UNITED STATES.

Weber, Brom, ed.
**O MY LAND, MY FRIENDS:
THE SELECTED LETTERS OF HART CRANE.**